Villages Nearby

A Story of Outreach in Alaska

Villages Nearby

A Story of Outreach in Alaska

by

Glen Lewis Van Dyne

Beacon Hill Press of Kansas City
Kansas City, Missouri

Unless otherwise indicated, all Scripture references are from *The Holy Bible, New International Version* (NIV), copyright © 1978 by the New York International Bible Society, and are used by permission.

Permission to quote from other copyrighted versions is acknowledged with appreciation:

The *New American Standard Bible* (NASB), © The Lockman Foundation, 1960, 1962, 1963, 1968, 1971, 1972, 1973, 1975, 1977.

The Living Bible (TLB), © 1971 by Tyndale House Publishers, Wheaton, Ill.

KJV—King James Version

10 9 8 7 6 5 4 3 2 1

Dedication

To Cheri and Peter, two PKs who suffer from H.S.S.* syndrome. They loved Alaska even before they saw it, and taught me to climb mountains.

And to Mary Jo, who loves wildflowers (including me). She bloomed where she was planted.

*High Sensation Seekers.

Contents

Introduction

Being up early is an exhilarating experience. It's the *getting* up which I find uninspiring. For a long time I tried to follow Jesus' example as recorded in Mark 1:35-38, "Very early in the morning, while it was still dark, Jesus got up, left the house and went off to a solitary place, where he prayed" (v. 35). It was not easy for me. I much preferred the "It is vain for you to rise up early" passage in Ps. 127:2, KJV.

But I wanted very much to have it said about me as a young pastor what Peter said about Jesus when he interrupted the Master's early morning prayer vigil: "Everyone is looking for you!" (v. 37). Somehow I had equated the discipline of early morning prayer meetings with great crowds waiting on my ministry.

Solitary wilderness places came to mean much to me early in life. Growing up on a farm in southeast Kansas afforded many opportunities to retreat to the woods and creeks of this near-Ozark country. Sunday afternoons were the best time to seek the restorative powers of nature with a hike alone in the hills and ravines of our farmstead. Places for contemplation could be found on the rocks of sandstone bluffs where Native American children used to play, or by the banks of Drum Creek, which flowed lazily along not far from our house.

As a preteen of 11 years, I came to know Jesus as my personal Friend in the forgiveness of sins. I began to seek my own early morning place of communion with God. There was a natural sandstone altar about halfway up a ravine which became my personal trysting place. So sacred was that spot that I did not reveal its significance to my closest relatives until I had long since grown to manhood and left the security of home and family. It was there that I first heard the call of God to preach the gospel. I dreamed of going to faraway places as a missionary to people with strange-sounding names and languages.

Often in the deepest part of the woods, where I was sure no one would see or hear me, I would find some vantage point on the side of a stream or hill and preach to the assembled "multitudes" who had come to hear me. Those early "crowds" numbered in the thousands! Someday, I knew, those trees and rocks would be real people.

When the days of preparation for my pastoral ministry were finished and I eagerly accepted my first assignment, the vision of "Everyone is looking for you!" began to dim a bit. "Multitude" was not a true descriptor of the "success" I was enjoying. Nevertheless I knew that in time the "crowds" would be there.

It was not until I literally went to the wilderness to pastor that I discovered verse 38 of that passage in Mark. All those years it had been my goal to be the kind of person who could attract a large following. Then one day in my sermon study I read, as for the first time, the reply of Jesus to Peter's urgent announcement of the waiting crowds. His answer penetrated my mind and heart with an insight that changed the course of my ministry. "Jesus replied, 'Let us go somewhere else—to the nearby villages—so I can preach there also. That is why I have come.'"

Finally I understood that my call to preach was not to be to large crowds but to small groups of people. It was not to be to distant lands and exotic peoples, but to those in my own native land.

This book is about the journey God allowed me to make to Eskimo and Indian villages while pastoring in Sitka, Alaska. My prayer is that you too will find your "villages nearby" and the adventure that waits you there as you follow Jesus.

—GLEN LEWIS VAN DYNE

1
Sunshine and Surf

Life was good for us in beautiful Santa Barbara, Calif. The climate was ideal. Mornings were cool and foggy with the sun breaking through the clouds between eight and ten o'clock, to reveal a sparkling blue Pacific.

The ocean was bounded by sandy beaches. Offshore islands were visible 20 miles or so across the channel. Days off were sometimes filled by accepting an invitation to go fishing for bonita. We had come to feel very much at home in this sophisticated, aristocratic community 100 miles northwest of Los Angeles. It was far enough out of L.A. to be free of smog, yet close enough for us to take advantage of the cultural events in the city.

Our children were doing well in school. Friends and fellow pastors encouraged us in our ministry.

For Mary Jo, living in California was the fulfillment of a long-held dream. When we moved to Los Angeles after four years of pastoring in Hawaii, she felt like she had come home at last. California for her was right next to heaven. Neatly manicured lawns and flowers the year round brought a sense of satisfaction and well-being to her artistic temperament. She felt content to remain here for the rest of her life.

This idyllic community in southern California was a good place to raise children. A short drive through the mountains took us past beautiful Lake Cachuma to the quaint Danish village of Solvang. We could drive the coastal highway past spectacular ocean vistas and secluded beaches. The area abounded in historical, cultural, social, recreational, and spiritual resources.

The years watching our children grow up were a delight to us. A large field back of the parsonage provided endless hours of play for Cheri and Peter. Learning to ride bicycles and horses, building sand castles on the beach, running in the surf, and flying kites occupied many happy hours.

Flying a small plane became one of my favorite hobbies. Taking off on a cool morning flight on the runway which extended toward the beach and open ocean was an exhilarating, spirit-lifting experience.

Whether walking at sunset on an isolated stretch of beach or having an early breakfast on the old wharf, there was much to enhance our life-style. We felt rich far beyond our modest pastor's salary and parsonage. We envied the lot of no one living elsewhere.

But then, we had never been poor in experience during any of the pastorates we had since I graduated from Nazarene Theological Seminary. Our first assignment was to help plant a new church in Boulder, Colo. This was followed with another challenge to dig out a church in Jonesboro, Ark.

Home Missions continued to be our calling as we went to Hawaii under Dr. Melza Brown. In that "paradise of the Pacific" a multiethnic congregation in Wahiawa began for us a love affair with cross-cultural ministries.

As a young pastor in Hawaii I gained valuable experience serving the district as NYPS president and Church School Board chairman. Memories of spiritually high youth camps and colorful Sunday morning worship services are still vivid in my mind. Only the continued severe illness of our Hawaiian-born son, Peter, caused us to leave that lovely clime to return to the mainland.

On a spectacularly beautiful day (just another ordinary day in Hawaii), loaded with love and leis, we bade farewell to our island home and friends to move to sunny, though sometimes smoggy, southern California.

Four years of pastoring in the Los Angeles community of Sun Valley preceded our move to Santa Barbara by the ocean. Extending our six-year stay there was appealing in the light of our many moves earlier in our ministry. But a restless spirit began to invade my heart.

It was not so much a discontent with where I was living as it was a feeling of slipping into a velvet-lined rut. This restlessness was aggravated by calls to other churches on the L.A. District. I properly considered them all in my willingness to leave this comfortable setting to accept a new challenge. But in my spirit I felt no clear direction to accept any of these opportunities.

2
A Voice in the Night

Saturdays are special in a parsonage. While most people are relaxing at repairing the family car, cutting the grass, picnicking, or doing those odd jobs that have been put off until this seventh day, the pastor and his family are caught up in the last-minute preparations for leading a congregation in worship.

Pace and pulse quicken as the responsibilities and opportunities of Sunday are anticipated. The climax of the week for the pastor comes on the first day. We had grown accustomed to this pattern.

And so it was that on a particular Saturday in June of 1974 preparations were completed for the coming day of worship. I retired early in order to be rested and fit for doing the best possible job when I met with the gathered congregation. Everyone was safe in bed. Sleep had come to bless us with its restorative powers.

The silent darkness of midnight was shattered with the urgent ringing of the telephone. Calls in the middle of the night are not unusual in a parsonage. They always signal some interesting, if not informative, experience. This one was to be life-changing.

It was Rev. Robert Sheppard, district superintendent of Alaska. He was calling from Sitka where the church board had come to the conclusion that we should be extended a call to be their next pastor. My first thought was, They certainly must be night owls in Alaska; I don't think I would fit. But I suppressed the thought and listened to Rev. Sheppard. In his kind, courteous way he asked me to think and pray about coming to Sitka. I agreed to do so.

Something about that phone call made sleep difficult the rest of the night. So we prayed, talked, and even cried a little at the idea of such a change in direction for our ministry. The prospect of living through a busy day of church activities without revealing this call was challenging indeed. We would find a way to cope with that. But one factor we had not reckoned on.

PKs (preacher's kids) have been endowed by their Creator with very sensitive ears. Cheri and Peter were no exceptions to this rule. So after lunch we were interrogated. Finally the content of the call was confessed. Excitement filled the air as these two adolescents tried to convince their father that this call was certainly the voice of God and he need not pray about it any longer. Peter was ready to pack his bags and leave before the evening service.

Parents are slower to catch on. It was several days before a decision was made, not without agony and deep heart-searching, that this was indeed God's call for us.

Let it be clearly understood that preachers who receive such calls are married to women who must often depend on the discernment of their husbands to know where God is leading them. Being a wife to such an adventurous sort was Mary Jo's lot in life.

While she was convinced that Alaska might be good for her husband and children, she failed to see how God could use her talents and abilities in that rugged, unknown frontier called Alaska. She viewed herself as one more suited to the amenities of city life than to the deprivations of the wilderness. Sitka's location on an island was not a positive factor in Mary Jo's thinking. A few years earlier the prospect of living in the Hawaiian Islands had frightened her; now the isolation of living on an island in the wilderness of Alaska was overpowering. Shades of Robinson Crusoe! There was no doubt about it—her poor husband was really "hearing voices" in the night.

When pressed for an answer to the ever-present question in her mind, "What does God want me to go to Alaska for, anyway?" I was without words. Finally I reasoned with her that although I did not understand all that God must have in mind, I was certain that He wanted something beautiful in Alaska or He wouldn't be asking us to go—I certainly wasn't going without her! So after long, animated discussions and tearful prayers, this dedicated, committed pastor's wife agreed to go "whither thou goest" (Ruth 1:16, KJV), even if this meant to the vast unknown territory called Alaska.

Announcement to the church of our intention to resign the pastorate in Santa Barbara and move to Sitka was followed by detailed preparation for going. Fellow Nazarene pastors supported our decision. Some seemed to speak with envy in their voices when we told them of trading southern California for the real and imagined rugged isolation of the Far North.

3
Journey Northward

The excitement of our new adventure was shared by the congregation at Santa Barbara. At a farewell church dinner the teens made giant signs and taped them to the wall of the fellowship hall. They were full of humor. Many of them literally came true as the trip unfolded.

There was one depicting us loaded into our Ford wagon with our dog, Coco, riding as a hood ornament showing Peter and Cheri hanging out the windows. Others illustrated the mission they envisioned for us. One such poster pictured a parka-clad pastor with an icicle hanging from his nose and a candle in his hand. It was entitled: "Bringing the light to Alaska."

Another prophetic poster showed us all on a ferryboat. This one was to come pleasantly true. Actually two ferryboats were our major means of transportation on the long trek north.

The first half of the journey was by car. We drove as far as the north part of Vancouver Island in beautiful British Columbia. There we took passage on a Canadian ferry for Prince Rupert. What it lacked in luxurious accommodations (our stateroom was below the waterline) was made up for by the hospitality of the crew and the excellent service. British Columbians certainly know how to make you one of the family.

An overnight stay in Prince Rupert gave us a chance to catch our breath and explore this semifrontier town. At this point the isolation and distance began to penetrate our minds and emotions. We caught our first sight of an eagle as we walked out of the hotel after breakfast.

The Alaska ferry *Malispina* was our final carrier. On this we had a comfortable, if confining, stateroom. Two double bunks, our own shower and commode made a cozy home for two days and a night on the water.

Traveling by ferry or steamship to Alaska is one of the most fascinating ways to move or vacation. The ferries do not offer the luxury of the tour ships, but it is easier to get the feeling of adventure on a ferry than on an ocean liner. Both offer a cruise with changing scenery as they move through the beautiful fjords bordering the Canadian mainland.

We enjoyed the restful journey by walking the deck in the crisp, cool, damp air. Spotting eagles, porpoises, and whales occupied many hours. There was time for letter writing, reading books, and leisurely enjoying meals in the lovely dining room.

The farther north we traveled, the longer the daylight lasted. Our senses became acutely aware of the immensity of the place to which we were going.

The last leg of the journey took us through fjords where the channel narrowed to scarcely the length of the vessel. Passage at either high or slack tide was necessary, otherwise the current would be flowing more rapidly than the speed of the ship. For this reason the ferry always stays in Sitka for at least three hours and on occasion for six in order to "go with the flow."

The emotions accompanying the slow approach to the final docking for us in Sitka were extremely mixed. Good portions of high excitement and fear of the unknown swept over us like the cold winds sweeping the deck. From safe and warm inside the cabin we watched as the tiny terminal facility came into view.

"I think there's a sign there for us!" Peter announced excitedly. Sure enough a little band of church members from the Sitka congregation had come to meet us. Their home-made sign took away any secrecy we might have hoped for in our arrival plans.

As we drove our car off the ferry and on to the solid earth of Baranof Island we were immediately surrounded by the happy faces of our new family.

Cheri Van Dyne standing on the bridge to Japonski Island; in the background is downtown Sitka and the mountains of Baranof Island.

The *Malispina* docked in Sitka on July 21, 1974. The physical journey was complete. It would take much longer to feel at home in this new land than it had taken to leave the sunshine of California and travel to the rain forest of southeast Alaska.

The water which washed on this new shore bore the same name as the waves which caressed the Santa Barbara beaches, but to our senses it was another planet.

My personal journal for July 26 reveals some of our feelings of apprehension in this seemingly alien place:

> The shock of being confined to so small an area is more than the southern California psyche can bear. Everything is extremely different to the senses. Looking out the window and seeing snow-capped mountain peaks similar to Switzerland (so I am told) dazzles my mind.
>
> Then there is the constant daylight or at least twilight. As I write this at 10:15 P.M. I can see the trees clearly on the mountains at the edge of town. This condition will last much of the night with the sun rising again shortly after 4 A.M. We have not yet conditioned ourselves to going to bed by the clock. Years of going to bed because of the darkness make a habit that is hard to break.

We soon discovered that what Sitka lacked in appearance compared to Santa Barbara's carefully manicured look, it made up in warm, loving people. Church members often greeted us with the question, "Is the rain getting to you?" They were concerned lest we become discouraged with the nearly constant rainfall. A normal year sees from 8 to 10 feet of rain.

When the initial shock had lessened a bit we determined to make the best of what at first had appeared to be a wrong choice. And so off we started. Walking in the rain. Using what we found. Fixing what we could. Learning to do without what we could not obtain. Overwhelmed by the needs for change we saw around us, nevertheless we started out to make an impact in this strange and wonderful land.

We were to find many more obstacles in the way of reaching our intended goals, but the battle was engaged. We were committed—outwardly at least. Problems were made to solve, right? Well, we had plenty of work cut out for us, this being the case.

4

The Only Way Out Is Up

True to form, our children adjusted to this new land much faster than we did. There was much to explore for a boy and girl who suffer from an H.S.S. syndrome (High Sensation Seekers). In spite of all our "There might be bears in the woods" warnings, they managed to get acquainted quickly with mountains, ocean, and local "natives."

The days grew noticeably short as September came and our sophomore and sixth grader were back in school. The clouds continued to drop rain and blot out the sunshine much of the time. But we were getting used to that. Another kind of cloud appeared on the horizon. The darkness it brought seemed impossible to dispel.

Saturday, September 21, the sun rose in a cloudless sky, but it was dark all day. The darkness was not in the atmosphere but in my heart. It was two months to the day from the time we arrived in Sitka. Coming to Alaska had been the fulfillment of a dream for 11-year-old Peter. Now he was lying in a hospital room, coughing his lungs out inside an oxygen tent, fighting for his life.

The darkness was accompanied by despair. We had tried everything humanly possible to stop the cough which had begun a week before. It only worsened. Now we were at the end of ourselves. Well, not quite at the end—that would come later.

Mary Jo and I went to the hospital at 9 A.M. after a few hours of fitful sleep to find that Peter had awakened at four o'clock that morning. He did not sleep again until 11 P.M. He was no better. The hospital staff was convinced that we should leave him alone, that we should go home. The doctor who had admitted him to the hospital was gone for the weekend and would not be back until the following Wednesday. His partner would be our doctor. This was the third doctor we had seen within a week's time. Panic rears its ugly head when you have seen all the doctors there are in the town and none offers much hope.

Friday morning a bronchoscope had revealed the presence of a rare bacteria. Treatment with injections was begun. Following the examination, Peter was put in the croup tent with cold moisture-laden air being pumped in. To us it only seemed to make matters worse. Nevertheless the doctor insisted on continuing this treatment.

To add to our frustration when we arrived at the hospital on Saturday morning, the croup tent motor was running, but the fresh air hose had become disconnected. This experience was repeated when we returned at four in the afternoon.

At this point of despair, I vented my frustration and anger to the hospital staff. One of the doctors came in and talked with us. We agreed there was nothing more the hospital treatment could do for Peter and decided to take him home.

With heavy hearts we gathered his things together and I carried him, like a baby, to the car. He coughed his way home and into his own bed. Now, at least his welfare was back in our own hands.

Saturday night he coughed himself to sleep again. Sunday was like the mornings had been for more than a week now—he awoke coughing. This continued throughout the day.

That Saturday evening we prayed, talked, and tried to decide what to do next. We checked the air fares to Santa Barbara, thinking that if he continued to show no improvement we would fly him there for treatment.

I went late that evening to my study to get some work done for Sunday. With a week of care and concern for Peter, I had done no sermon preparation. Mary Jo came down and we talked for a few minutes; the tears came as I tried to pray.

It seemed to our minds impossible to understand that God would so clearly bring us here and then allow this to be the end of it. After Mary Jo had gone from my office I thought about the fact that Isa. 43:3 was still in the Bible. I knew in my mind that God was a Man of His Word. Still, I had to come to the end of myself and say, "Lord, I don't understand this. I know You are not the kind of person who would bring us to this place and leave us. Please help us, O God, please help us now!"

Sunday was a day filled with paradoxes. Peter's coughing continued. I was unprepared to lead the service. It was the day for the annual Sunday School dinner, so there was a record number in attendance. The sanctuary was packed and overflowing for the worship service. I found myself preaching about the love of God. We closed the morning service with the singing of the hymn:

> O Love that wilt not let me go,
>   I rest my weary soul in Thee.
> I give Thee back the life I owe,
> That in Thine ocean depths its flow
>   May richer, fuller be.
>
> O Joy that seekest me through pain,
>   I cannot close my heart to Thee.
> I trace the rainbow through the rain,

And feel the promise is not vain
That morn shall tearless be.

I came home too exhausted to make much effort in preparation for the evening service. In my journal I recorded this thought:

> I must say that I have learned the lesson here that this work is God's and not mine. He wants to do it through me. I have only to provide the willing tool through which He can work. When I rest in the Lord, He is able to work far better than when I frantically fuss around trying to see that everything is going just like I think it should. I have come so many times to the end of my resources, and the job is not half done. I have had to say again and again, "Lord, unless You do it, it won't be done at all."

Earlier in the day I had tried in vain to call the district superintendent in Anchorage. Weather conditions prevented the radio-signal phone contact from being completed. To add to the feeling of helplessness we found out that the one southbound and one northbound plane a day were unable to land because of the weather. The clouds were literally on the ground. Under no circumstances could we take Peter to Seattle or Santa Barbara. Even Juneau and Anchorage were beyond our reach. Feelings of isolation and helplessness like we have never known before gripped our hearts. The fog blanketing Baranof Island all day Sunday was not half as thick as the fog blanketing our hearts.

When the time came for the evening service, I walked into a full sanctuary to be enfolded in music, testimonies, and praise. God spoke through us about the ministry of the Holy Spirit as Presence. There was a warm and good response.

When the last person was greeted and an informal youth meeting was ended after the evening service, I went up the hill a few steps in the misting rain to the parsonage.

About ten o'clock Mary Jo came into the living room

where I was sitting exhausted from the activities and care of the day. She broke down and cried and prayed as she sat on the sofa. I knelt by her side and prayed quietly in a mood of despair.

On Monday I stayed with Peter during another day of coughing. Mary Jo spent most of the day working in the church's day-care center. The doctor convinced us we should wait through one more night, and then he would consult with doctors in Seattle by phone.

As soon as she walked in the door at 5:30 in the evening, Mary Jo said to me, "He's not coughing anymore!" Almost immediately Peter got out of bed, came into the living room, and asked if he could go outside and play on a rope swing on the tree in our front yard. We began to praise God for deliverance! Peter ate a meal, played some, and went to bed. In the morning he slept late and to all evidences was well. In my journal I noted:

> Now I have written all this down so I will not forget that the God who leads also keeps watch over us.
>
> Isa. 43:2-3 is still in the Bible: "When you go through deep waters and great trouble, I will be with you. When you go through rivers of difficulty, you will not drown! When you walk through the fire of oppression, you will not be burned up—the flames will not consume you. For I am the Lord your God" (TLB).
>
> No doubt there will be other times when darkness descends, the waters rise, and the flames surround. Then we will remember the God who never leaves nor forsakes.

Mary Jo shared with me the moment when the end of the struggle about Peter came for her. She was in the day-care center helping two new girls get started in their work. It was nap time for the children. She was sitting between two of them rubbing their backs. As she thought about the children who have come to be her ministry she remembered what she knew of them.

One child had been so severely beaten by his parents he was a cripple. He was no longer allowed to live with his mother and father. Another was a child whose father had recently been killed in the sinking of a barge. Still another had a father who was imprisoned for murder, and the child had accidentally killed another child with an "unloaded" gun.

Several years before, when he was an infant and we were living on the island of Oahu, Hawaii, Peter lay in the intensive care unit of a small hospital with a high fever and convulsions. That was the first time Mary Jo came to the place of releasing her son into the hands of a God who knows better than parents how to care for children.

Sitting there among these children and thinking about her own son, she felt a release in her heart and said, "OK, Lord, he's in Your hands!"

It was almost at that exact moment Peter stopped coughing and dramatically improved. In the space of an hour he was well!

This was a very real experience; I have not exaggerated the facts. Never in my life have I gone through such deep despair and seen in the midst of it the hand of my loving Heavenly Father at work in spite of what I was feeling or thinking.

In my journal I wrote this prayer: "Lord, don't ever let me forget what You have done for us. Thank You for the experience of Peter's illness. Teach me how to share Your love and care with others in this place where the isolation, loneliness, and frustration sometimes blot out the sun."

Before we left Santa Barbara, the teens joked with us about bringing the light to Alaska. But that is exactly what happened in our own lives.

The weather clouds often came all the way down to the ground, blotting out the lovely landscape which surrounded us. But because we had already seen Sitka bathed in the beauty of sun and sea, we knew that even when the clouds blotted everything out, the mountains were still there, the ocean still ebbed and flowed, and above it all the sun was still shining!

In 1983 Peter made a solo bicycle trip from Florence, Oreg., to Yorktown, Va., without illness or mishap.

5
The Last Frontier

The State of Alaska is lovingly called "The Great Land" by "sourdoughs" and "natives." ("Sourdoughs" are old-timers in Alaska. "Native" is a reference to ethnicity rather than birthplace.) Alaska is a state of indescribable extremes.

Impossible to capture by either camera lens or printed page, this 49th state defies description, yet invites everyone's curiosity to come and explore. Once people do, they are caught in a web from which there is little hope of release, though they travel far and wide from this mysterious, fascinating land.

Anthropologists tell us Alaska was the point of land on which ancient peoples set foot when they had crossed the then existing land bridge between what is now known as Siberia and Alaska. There is archaeological evidence to support this theory.

History reminds us of the discovery of this vast area by early Russian explorers. They left their mark on the land and sea with fur trading expeditions and explorations. Most notable among the landmarks from that era are the still active Russian Orthodox churches in Alaskan villages and the Cathedral in Sitka.

"Seward's Folly" is the phrase which conjures up memories of the purchase of Alaska from the Russians in 1867. Each year this historical occasion is reenacted on Alaska Day, October 18. Two cents an acre seems like a small price now to have paid for this magnificent piece of real estate.

In the hundred years since the purchase from the Russians, most of the land has remained uncharted. It is a wilderness preserved more by nature than by government decree.

Gold rushes, oil strikes, and fishing have all played important parts in the development of this far north land which still wears the title "The Last Frontier" honestly.

Thousands of people have called Alaska home over the years. Each year more come and go, trying their luck and skills against the harsh environments in both bush and city. Most of the population centers in Anchorage and surrounding area. But the remote, isolated villages and communities of the state comprise another Alaska. Even the capital, Juneau, has a unique atmosphere as a former gold rush town. Its isolation is highlighted by the fact that often the state lawmakers cannot get a flight in or out of the town because of the inclement weather.

There is a variety of climate across the thousands of miles between north and south, east and west. From the "banana belt" of the southeast where rain is measured in feet rather than inches; to the stark plains of Point Barrow on the north shore of the subcontinent where snow is as common as sunshine in Florida; to the 60-below wintertime temperatures of the interior around Fairbanks; to the fog-shrouded and wind-swept Aleutian chain of islands, weather is a common foe of Native Alaskan and sourdough alike. You learn to live with it, or you get out of the state. Learning to live with it can be a herculean task defeating the most experienced wilderness folks.

The scenery is spectacular. It surrounds you like stereophonic music. In every direction you can turn in most rural areas there is a panorama of natural beauty untouched by civilization's debris.

Sitka by the Sea

The spirit of the old Russian settlement still lingers in this modern bush-village, yet cosmopolitan, Alaskan city. Older than San Francisco, it has an influence far in excess of its small size of around 8,000 souls. Here, every October 18, the transfer of the territory of Alaska from Russia to the United States is re-created in a pageant on top of Castle Hill, the very spot where the original ceremony took place.

Sitka is on an island about 100 miles long and varying in width from 15 to 20 miles. Thousands of miles of coastline are created by innumerable inlets and bays. It is topped with glacier-draped mountains up to 5,000 feet above sea level. The Pacific Ocean caresses it on all sides. Tall spruce trees

Sitka viewed from halfway up Mount Verstovia. Mount Edgecumbe is on the horizon.

cover most of the land from the high tide to the snow level. Isolated. Rainy. Crowded in between the mountains and the sea, it will always be isolated as far as transportation is concerned.

To describe the people living here requires the use of terms such as: Tlingit (clink-it) Indian, Russian Orthodox, logger, fisherman, government employee, educator, Coast Guard, student, tourist. Sitka has seen the coming and going of many eras. The Russians left a certain sophistication and austerity. To this mystical fantasy island, the tourists love to come and pretend they are witnessing an old and faraway time.

The Americans came and continued the attempt at subduing the people and the land. But Sitka and Baranof Island are not the kind of places easily changed. They maintain a kind of studied indifference to all attempts at the subjugation which various ages have tried to impose on them. Sitka will always be uniquely Sitka. Even the modern improvements of hotels and paved streets leave relatively untouched the atmosphere of this community, self-sufficient yet connected with all the world.

Sitka Church of the Nazarene

A relative newcomer, the Church of the Nazarene appeared on the Sitka scene just three years before Alaska attained statehood in 1959. It was started in the home of a schoolteacher at Mount Edgecumbe. A house across the street from the campus at the Presbyterian-founded Sheldon Jackson College was the first meeting place. When the meetings outgrew the living room, more space was found in the local Carpenter's Hall on Monastery Street. Continued growth called for a move to the Seventh Day Adventist church building on Sawmill Creek Road.

The people who came were a typical mixture from the community: military personnel from the Coast Guard vessel;

teachers from Mount Edgecumbe Bureau of Indian Affairs High School; community professional and nonprofessional working people; workers in the fishing industry; and children from white and Indian families who made up the community. Soon the little building was crowded out.

The opportunity came to buy a portion of ground near the old Russian cemetery. So it came about that the Sitka Church of the Nazarene found a permanent physical home on a hillside overlooking Swan Lake and the main intersection of roadways on the island. Seven miles to the north the highway ended near the Alaska ferry terminal. Seven miles to the south it terminated at the site of the Japanese-owned pulp mill. On this historic site the church continued to grow. A parsonage was built, the first unit of the church was constructed and soon was filled to capacity.

In the first 25 years of its history the church in Sitka saw five men serve as pastors. Times of service ranged from a few months to nearly eight years.

It has always been a cross-cultural congregation, attracting people of all the ethnic groups in the community and from various denominational backgrounds as well. The Church of the Nazarene was for a long time the only holiness church there. Those who came looking for a live, growing, loving fellowship were drawn to this church on the hillside built of wood which blended in with the tall spruce trees dominating the old cemetery. In contrast to the cemetery behind the church, the town volunteer fire department building stood on the street below.

Nazarenes in Sitka felt more affinity for firetrucks than tombstones. There is a warm spirit in the simple, open-beam chapel where the congregation meets. Nothing about the building is elaborate or expensive by outside standards. Most of the building has been built by the loving hands of members of the congregation.

Through the incessant rains they come to worship and

fellowship. Some part of the building is used daily. Alabaster funds made possible the first unit, proving to be a sound investment yielding a high rate of return.

The often crowded sanctuary has been remodeled several times. It is not particularly well designed. There is no side room to the platform for choir and minister to enter. There is no spacious foyer for visiting after church services, so the aisles and pews become places for informal fellowship. There is a kitchen which is woefully inadequate for the many fellowship dinners the congregation finds so necessary in a community where social interaction is vital to survival. When more than 100 people are present for a dinner, which is most of the time, they must eat in two different rooms and often spill over into the sanctuary. It is truly a building with every room a multipurpose one.

Sitka Church of the Nazarene in the winter

Such is the frontier on which God allowed us to serve from 1974 to 1982. There we discovered "new frontiers" we had no idea existed in our own lives.

6
One Day at a Time

For more than 20 years I have kept a journal in the form of a rather intimate talk with God on paper. Usually these were recorded in the mornings. They were written without any thought of sharing them with anyone beyond my wife. If you have read this book this far, you are going to get a chance now to look deeper into my heart as I recall some of the events and emotions of those first months in Alaska.

Two reasons prompt me to do this: (1) I want you to get the feeling of being there with me so that when you encounter similar experiences they won't seem so strange to you. Looking back now, I can see clearly how the hand of God was on our lives. (2) If it encourages you to keep some kind of daily record of your experiences and encounters with the moving of the Spirit of God in your life, then I will be pleased.

Here goes:

October 6, 1974

"Keep Jesus movin'." With those words a young Eskimo college student from Sheldon Jackson College introduced his singing of the folk song "Pass It On." He sang it softly to the accompaniment of his guitar.

It was gently amusing when he spoke it, but on this morning after, I have been unable to remove the prod of this truth from my mind. I must keep Jesus moving. He must be passed on. Jesus cannot be kept safe and compartmentalized in my own life. I must share Him or I will lose Him.

I must go again to the Gospel of Mark where I see Jesus moving through the multitudes and into the towns and villages. He was constantly on the move as He lived among us. He was moving out to where the people were with real needs, and He was doing something about those needs.

So often I am tempted to find a nice, comfortable place in life and get a little soft nest made where I can have a cozy Christianity and not be disturbed by the battle of life and lives which goes on outside. This is not what Jesus wants. He wants to be kept moving.

Could it be that this is what God is saying to me by throwing me out of comfortable nests I have made for myself?

"Lord, thanks for the unsettlings You send my way. You know that I wouldn't do any growing or any sharing if it were not for this pushing me out."

October 11, 1974

"This is Alaska." That is given as an explanation for many things in this "far north" country. Here you have to learn to do with what you have or do without. This explains some of the strange things found in house construction and in automobiles. (For a while we owned a car with no reverse gear in it. Some people thought it quite appropriate for a preacher. They called it a "One-Way-mobile." I never backed up for anybody.—I did get into some pretty interesting situations at times.)

All the man-produced material things are soon in a state of disrepair. They remain that way for life because there is no easy way to get repairs or to find replacements. One goes on using them or fixes them the best way he can; or, if worst comes to worst, he discards them and does without.

Yet, in spite of this status quo, I find myself keeping on hoping and working for a better state of affairs. I am not satisfied with the cluttered look of the church property. I hope in another six months to have things looking better. I must keep on pushing to accomplish this feat.

"Lord, don't let me be poured into the mold of the world around me.

"In the name of Jesus, who was able to accomplish all that the Father sent Him to do."

October 19, 1974

We learned to appreciate sunshine today. The sun finally broke through the clouds which have dropped rain upon this land for more than two weeks, almost without a moment's hesitation.

It was different from the experience of breaking through the clouds in an airplane to the brilliance of sunlight above. It is something else to have the clouds parted and the sunshine reach all the way down to the wet earth on which we walk. Now we truly know what the poet meant to express when he wrote, "And sunlight is the sweeter after rain."

Peter expressed it most positively when he said this evening, "We saw *five* rainbows today, not just one!" Our dinnertime was interrupted by the sight out the living room window of a brilliant rainbow rising out of Swan Lake and ending on the college campus across town. The arch became the playground of white-winged sea gulls diving and soaring in the late evening sun. In the background the mountain peaks of the Three Sisters and Arrowhead were taking off their thin veil of clouds to reveal pure-white mantles of newly fallen snow. We tried—vainly, I'm sure—to capture the sight and experience on film. Moments like that are something to hold on to forever; they make us forget the weeks of rain and gray, cloud-filled skies.

37

"Thank You, Lord, for letting the sunshine break through the clouds."

October 23, 1974

The prelude is past. This is the real thing. I feel the town, the church, and everyone who knows we are here is now ready to see just what we can do. Only by the grace of God will we do what He has sent us to do.

The biggest rain in several years has let up for a few hours. We have been subjected to several tests of the spirit already, and I am certain more will come. "Lord, make us strong to bear them and to realize Your strength in the midst of and through to the end—the victorious end of them."

October 25, 1974

The rain ever comes. It never stops. There has got to be an end somewhere. Each morning it is the same—slow but steady drizzle. It is beginning to hurt to see the children go off to school in the rain and darkness. Still life goes on. We do not stop and wait for the sunshine here. We simply trust that the sun is shining above these clouds. It will burst through one of these mornings, and we'll all rise up singing.

Indoors is a bright world in such weather. The warmth of a bright and dry room becomes meaningful. This contrast with the bright sunshine of the out-of-doors we experienced for so long in southern California is making the adjustment more difficult. Yet, we must not wish for the sun of California here any more than we would wish for the rain of southeast Alaska there.

God has put us here for a purpose, and we will live out that purpose for as long as He asks us to stay. "Lord, give me a peace about being here, and give us the supply for all our needs. We do claim Your promises for us and for this place."

November 18, 1974

It's nice to come to a warm, well-lighted, orderly office with windows looking out on the main street in this small Alaskan village-town. Right now there is a mixture of snow and rain falling. The weather speaks of winter getting serious about staying here for a while. The snow comes farther down the mountainsides daily. A new crispness is in the air, and I pull my parka zipper up a little higher these days when I walk downtown.

November 20, 1974

Since morning the soft, feathery, fluffy stuff has been coming down, covering Sitka with snow. Cheri said it in the car on the way to school this morning—"It makes things look better, doesn't it?"

November 21, 1974

Just yesterday the first real snow of the season fell on Sitka. It remains on the ground this morning to greet the sun which is racing the clouds returning for more moisture to pour on our land and sea.

This first snow was beautiful to behold. As in Sonny Salisbury's song, "The snow makes everything new." It covers all the ugly scars man has made on the landscape.

Now with the brilliant arctic sun sending its rays at a low angle across the landscape, the earth around me sparkles with a thousand million diamonds more lovely than anything man can fashion. "God, You really know how to make things beautiful. Thanks!"

On days like this I want to be a poet. I do not want to engage in any mundane tasks of daily living. Yet, those same tasks can be done with new inspiration. Where in all the world can such a lovely setting be found in which to work?

Many times I complain about the weather here. I must learn to be grateful for the variety we have in forms of moisture. We could not long survive without water.

So much for the weather report. I just wanted you to get the feel of 10 feet of rain a year.

The beginning of a new calendar year seemed to mark a turning in attitude, as revealed in this journal entry for January 3, 1975:

39

Here at the threshhold of the year I have a simple desire. I want to excel in the common, ordinary, daily living tasks. I long for no great accomplishments as much as I long for success in the everyday details of life. True, I would like to be able this year to write in a fulfilling way. However, I believe that noble accomplishment will come only as I care for the daily tasks which are my responsibility to perform.

Six months had passed since we arrived in Alaska. Life was coming into focus. Here in the dead of winter when the days were extremely short and the nights dark, cold, and only good for staying indoors, a serenity was settling down upon our emotions.

A busy round of activities in the church and community was enveloping our lives. School for the children held good things.

In the church we were beginning to get a music program going. Even though there was not any provision in the building for a choir, we started one and made plans for making room.

The sanctuary had been enlarged in the remodeling/expansion project which we completed after we arrived. Already the pews were filled on many occasions, and we wondered what they did before we came.

I was beginning to think in terms of a ministry of the church in the community that would reach out beyond the walls of this building set on the hillside.

Thoughts of making contact with the community through radio programs, coffeehouses, and home church meetings were knocking around in my head.

7

Mr. Nutting and the Adoption Program

When most people think of Alaska they think of vast wilderness areas; grizzly bears; big fish; dogsleds; oil pipelines; GOLD; extreme cold; huge glaciers; whales; seals; walruses. Such thinking is not necessarily erroneous. But when I think of Alaska, I think of people. Not a lot of people, to be sure. There are right at a half million residents in the entire 7 million acres. That has to come out as more natural resources than people.

You may be attracted to vacation in this new frontier because of its natural beauty. You would not be disappointed. It would doubtless be worth the time and money. But you would miss the real Alaska if you didn't take time to get to know its people. They are the resource far more valuable than all the oil and gold and animals.

Most of Alaska's people are "imported." That is, their cultural roots are not there. They were drawn by some irresistible urge to come and see. They liked what they saw and stayed. Such folks are called "sourdoughs."

Less than one-fourth of the population fit the term "Native." Let me give you a helpful hint for your visit to Alaska. Don't ask anyone who is clearly a white Anglo if they are a "Native Alaskan." I won't predict their response. Hopefully they will kindly tell you that a "Native Alaskan" is a term reserved, respectfully, for the "original Alaskans." These are the Eskimo and Indian people who have so graciously allowed us sourdough-types to live among them.

Would you like to meet some of these unique one-of-a-kind people? Let me introduce one.

We will have to take a short drive, walk, or bicycle ride across the suspension bridge which connects Baranof Island to Japonski Island. Japonski is partly man-made since the ocean had to be filled in to accommodate the present 6,500-foot jet runway. It is home for the U.S. Coast Guard air station. The pier where the Coast Guard buoy-tender is docked is also there. The Bureau of Indian Affairs hospital has a home on this island. Alaska Airlines terminal is the scene of much coming and going with several flights daily. (More in the summer than in the winter.)

Mount Edgecumbe High School, a Bureau of Indian Affairs school, occupied a site on Japonski Island for years. It was housed in buildings which were built hastily during World War II for military personnel. They were not meant to last nearly as long as they have. With lots of care and money they have stood to serve the cause of education far longer than they served the cause of war.

In the 1980s Mount Edgecumbe High School was being phased out in favor of village schools. One of the persons who viewed this change with mixed emotions is a certain math teacher named Rod Nutting.

Rod came to Alaska from Washington. He grew up in Yakima. Sheldon Jackson College was the magnet that drew him. Actually it was the basketball coaching job at SJC which brought the Nuttings, Rod and Faye, to live on Baranof Island in southeast Alaska. After a few years as coach, he felt led of the Lord to accept a job at the BIA school across the bridge. Thus began his love affair with the Mount Edgecumbe High School students. It was destined to have far-reaching effects on his life and on the lives of hundreds of students and their families.

Teaching math and coaching the championship girls basketball team were the things for which he received a salary. But, like others who taught at this school, Rod did many things for which money could not adequately repay—nor would he have accepted it had it been offered. They were labors of love. Love for God translated into Eskimo, Athabascan, Aleut, and Tlingit students.

I would find Rod during class hours on the second floor of the old Navy hangar. From his window he could look across the narrow channel to Baranof Island and on lunch hours watch the traffic of fishing boats mixed with bush planes on floats.

It was a rare noon hour break which did not find "Mr. Nutting," as he was respectfully called, counseling at least one student. These young Eskimos and Indians were drawn to this blunt-spoken *gussick* (Eskimo name for person with pale white skin) whose humor they came to understand as he came to understand their culture.

The burden of Rod's heart was to bring these students to know Christ as Savior. To this end he expended uncounted hours after class and on weekends transporting them around Sitka in his blue, half-broken-down, Dodge pickup. Many a student learned the elementary lessons for driving in that old truck.

My first recollections of Rod are a Sunday afternoon climb up Mount Verstovia and Mount Arrowhead (a 3,500-foot climb from sea level).

We had only been in Sitka a month. All of a sudden one Sunday morning, unannounced to me, shortly after the morning worship service had begun, 50 dark-haired, blue-

43

denim-jacketed Eskimo boys and girls of high school age filed into the pews. Each one appeared to my wondering eyes to be a carbon copy of the next. I had not been prepared to meet Eskimos this far south in Alaska. They were supposed to be much farther north, I thought. And I was right, except for the fact that these were some of the 400-plus high school students from across the bridge.

That Sunday afternoon hike proved to be more than many of the students had bargained for. Most of them were from the part of Alaska which is treeless and flat. Now they faced the steep, tree-covered slopes of Mount Verstovia. Some of those trees were already giants when the Russians first settled there in the 18th century.

However, in typically quiet, uncomplaining Eskimo fashion they joined the climb on that beautiful sunny Sunday afternoon. It normally would take no longer than two hours up and two down. They started as a group. Like other climbs loosely organized and made up of a mixture of novice and expert climbers, they soon separated as the stronger, more experienced ones climbed faster.

About two-thirds of the way up the mountain I heard a plaintive cry echoing across the mountainside, "Mr. Nutting, Mr. Nutting!" Now I knew that "Mr. Nutting" was nowhere within earshot. I highly suspected that the Eskimo girl calling out in her lostness on the mountain knew he could not hear. But she had not known me long enough to remember my name or to feel free to speak to me, so she called out for help in the name of the only friend she knew. Perhaps just saying his name would bring help.

Sensing the plight of this flatland Eskimo, overwhelmed on this tree-covered mountain, I answered and assisted her in finding the way down the mountainside.

That is how I became aware of the influence of this young white math teacher-coach on the quiet, shy Native Americans from far, far north.

Rod's concern for these students was contagious. It became the spark for what came to be known as the "annual adoption service." Every September from 40 to 60 of these teens were welcomed into the hearts and homes of the congregation at the Sitka Church of the Nazarene.

Most of them never heard of the Nazarene church back in their home villages. Through the efforts of this layman, others in the congregation and community were involved in a project which provided a school bus to transport them to church services and activities. The local owner of the school bus and tour bus system, Mr. Gene Pruitt, donated the use of a bus any time Rod needed it for church activities involving the students.

At first the members of the congregation thought they were a beautiful curiosity as they came and sat in silent rows of reverence. Their shy smiles soon captured the hearts of the nonnatives in the church, and they sought to establish some kind of communication with them.

It was during the time when Rev. Al Haynes was pastor that the idea of an annual "adoption" Sunday was born. The plan was to invite the students who had chosen the church as their "church away from home" during the school year to be a member of a family in the congregation while they were in Sitka. Invitations to family activities, special occasions, and Sunday dinner became common as the bridge between the white community and the Eskimo-Indian community began to be built.

At first the students were not sure about the rather overpowering friendliness of the members of the mostly white congregation. But, like the melting of an iceberg with the warmth of summer sun and warm ocean currents, there began to emerge a communion and communication which was beautiful to behold and even more beautiful to experience.

Two cultures began to blend into a creation of beauty and blessing as real family ties were formed. The gen-

45

uineness of these "adoptions" was verified when Sitka families received long-distance phone calls (collect, of course—do children call any other way?) from distant Eskimo villages, "just because I wanted to talk to you." Parents in Sitka who had "adopted" students soon found themselves being called "Mom" and "Dad" by these lovely people who had welcomed us into their land.

Across the years the ties grew stronger. Letters were exchanged. When flying through Sitka, former students who had been a part of this program would stop off to spend a day or two with their Sitka "family." Birthdays were shared. New food became a part of the diet of both student and adoptive family.

A Sunday morning worship service in September was devoted to the adoption ceremony. Variations were made on the service from year to year. Once the television camera

Some Mount Edgecumbe High School students being honored at a reception for graduating seniors in the Sitka Church of the Nazarene.

recorded the meeting at the front of the church as students and family were introduced to each other and the entire congregation.

Families were invited to the school for special occasions. Graduation time became a heartwarming experience as students had the opportunity to bring together their two families—the one from the village and the one from Sitka. Many warm embraces took the place of conversations between two cultures and two families, each of which did not understand the language of the other. Smiles spoke volumes as each family made attempts to communicate thanks for the blessings which this special relationship had brought.

And so the bridge across the channel from Baranof to Japonski Island became a symbol of a more meaningful and lasting bridge between cultures, languages, and other barriers which often keep us apart.

Now that the school is closing down and the "adoption" program is officially over, it is clear that other ways will have to be found to keep the channel of communication open. Doubtless this will be one bridge no one wants to burn behind them.

8

Dan Etulain and ACTS-TV

In order to get to the heart of what this book is all about, you will have to meet another Alaskan sourdough. I'll need to point him out to you because he doesn't exactly fit the stereotype.

Dan Etulain is a Spanish Basque sheepherder's son. He has a Ph.D. in education and a built-in love for communications. What we have here is a case of a layman with a cross-cultural ministry. His heart has a large capacity for loving Native Americans, especially those living in his adopted state.

The Northwest was his home until that eventful summer when, with his wife, Kathie, he moved to Sitka to become a dedicated member of the faculty at Sheldon Jackson College. Prior to that, he had served his alma mater, Northwest Nazarene College, as dean of students. He accepted the position at SJC in order to be a part of a mission as an educator. (Sheldon Jackson College was founded by an early Presbyterian missionary shortly after the United States purchased the territory from Russia.)

Some people describe Dan as a "workaholic." The definition fits him in many ways. But he is one of the most optimistic and positive addicts to hard work I have met. To Dan there is no such thing as an idea that won't work, given time and a friendly atmosphere in which to grow. It has to be an idea that will help someone, or it doesn't find a welcome in his thinking. He is not so naive but what he can usually screen out in the beginning ideas that won't work. But even this he does so skillfully that the person who may have presented the idea feels complimented in the process of being turned down.

Organized confusion seems to be the atmosphere in which Dan works best, or so one might surmise from the looks of his office. But what his desk lacks in orderliness, his mind seems to make up in the ability to assimilate information when needed.

If Dan is guilty of loving his work so that he could spend hours on the job, he is not guilty of a lack of love for his lovely wife, Kathie, and sons, Todd and Troy. They are a busy family. But they are a family in the best sense of the word. This family life has been bought at the high price of taking time with each other, being active participants in the local Church of the Nazarene, and working out compromises necessary when both husband and wife are filling executive roles outside the home. Somehow they seem to have a sense of what is most important, and no matter how busy they are with jobs, there is adequate attention paid to the really important times and events in their lives.

Sunday will find the Etulains worshiping with the congregation in the brown wooden building at the corner of Halibut Point and Sawmill Creek roads. Their investment there is substantial. Serving on the church board, teaching Sunday School classes, being the church treasurer, and working at volunteer labor when there is a workday are all part of the commitment the Etulains have to their church and pastor. There is no less than 100 percent support of the work God is doing through that relatively small congregation by Dan and Kathie.

It is difficult to describe how the vision for reaching out to the small, isolated rural villages of Alaska came to Dan. I do know that in the summer of 1977 he began to write to me while he was on vacation "outside." He wanted my thoughts and prayers on the idea of using television to communicate with students and their families from Mount Edgecumbe High School and Sheldon Jackson College after they went back home to the village thousands of miles away from Sitka.

Some of it was born out of the defeat of another idea. From the ashes of a failure to obtain a grant from the state of Alaska for some educational television project, Dan began to build a phoenix of an idea for a ministry which could reach with the Good News into every community in Alaska in his own lifetime.

So I listened and wrote to this man who would not be silent about the burden God was placing on his heart.

During the first PALCON on the campus of Northwest Nazarene College, we arranged a meeting with Dr. Raymond W. Hurn from the office of Church Extension Ministries in Kansas City.

In an August summer-heated corner of the dining hall we spent a few minutes with Dr. Hurn, who was open and cordial to the idea. He offered advice and encouragement. A letter was written to Paul Skiles in the Department of Communications to solicit advice and, if possible, support.

Moss-covered southeast Alaska is a part of Alaska which most people overlook. But God has put it into the hearts of a few people like Dan and Kathie and others in the Sitka Church of the Nazarene to look upon it as the most important spot in the world.

Upon his return from vacation, Dan announced to me that he was going to go to the bank and open an account with $10.00 for this new ministry he believed God wanted us to form. That was the beginning step of faith which resulted in a nonexistent organization having its own bank account. The organization was soon to follow.

That fall there was a meeting in my study one weeknight. A few members of the congregation were invited to listen as Dan opened his heart with ideas for a ministry which would be an extension of the local church into all of Alaska. Serious questions were asked and hard facts were faced. Those present included: Lee Demmert (Tlingit Indian), the recently hired superintendent of Mount Edgecumbe; Rod and Fay Nutting; Grace Schoel, wife of a U.S. Coast Guard helicopter commander who was stationed in Sitka; Russ Wright (Tlingit Indian), a foreman of the Alaska Lumber and Pulp Mill and a member of the city council; Phyllis Moore (Eskimo); and Glen Van Dyne, pastor of the church.

The group talked about what such an organization could be called for identification purposes. Someone suggested ACTS 29, which had been the theme of the pastor's sermons for nearly a year. Finally it was agreed at the suggestion of Pastor Van Dyne to call it ACTS-TV for Alaska Christian Television Services To Villages.

With mixed feelings and probably little realization of what they had done, the little group prayed and were dismissed to go home in the cold, gentle rain. Thus it was that Dan Etulain became the instrument for the birth of an idea which has seen the hand of God over it in miraculous ways.

Nothing which could really be called spectacular, but a steady, continual, plodding growth has been characteristic of this mission which began out of frustration with a failure. It was nurtured in the context of a church at worship and work in a small, relatively inaccessible community on an island in cloud-blanketed southeast Alaska.

In the meantime, Dan continued to work at SJC and care for the dream in every spare moment he could find. His position at the college made it possible for him to be in contact with people at the state government level concerning the development of a television satellite system which would link all of Alaska's remote villages together with video. He saw this as a part of God's plan for the ministry of the ACTS-TV production company. It became his goal to be in on the ground floor, offering Alaskan-made Christian television before anyone else.

It is this forward-looking vision which has enabled this small beginning and this miniscule-funded operation to be there when the opportunities presented themselves.

Encouraged by a $500 grant from the Department of Communications/Church of the Nazarene, the baby production company began the ambitious project of a pilot program.

With equipment borrowed from Sheldon Jackson College, a Sunday afternoon was set aside for the first attempt. A group of eight Eskimo girls from Mount Edgecumbe were recruited to come to the church and sing in front of the camera. Furniture was moved from the platform, and the girls were seated on wooden stools and the carpeted floor. So the first videotape was recorded with singing by these students, mostly from the village of Tuntatuliak (tune-ta-tu-lee-ack). They were ideal performers, waiting patiently for long periods while these gussick amateur television producers fiddled with their camera, lights, and recorder until everything was working properly at the same time.

But I have strayed from the subject of the man who first cradled the idea of ACTS-TV.

Dan insisted on meeting regularly with his pastor to nurture the plan. His never-ending stream of ideas and concepts were carefully scrutinized by this sometimes skeptical pastor who was reluctant to be dragged into spending time working with media he knew precious little about.

Slowly, and with volumes of correspondence and publicity materials keeping the account low at the bank with postage expenditures, the story was shared with others. Anyone who would listen or ask questions was inundated with the reports and plans of this man with a dream to go to every village in Alaska with the Good News.

Now Dan is not really well equipped for life in Alaska. His idea of roughing it is watching a football game on TV *without* a can of his favorite soft drink in his hand. He could get more mileage out one can of Tab than a Honda gets from a gallon of gasoline.

His lack of natural adaptation to Alaska shows up in another realm. In order to get to the on-site recording places ACTS-TV must travel to, it is necessary to fly by small, single-engine bush planes and land on dirt/mud strips near the villages. Not one to relish even airline travel, flying these non-747-type airplanes prompted him to invest in wholesale lots of motion sickness medicines. This proved to be a self-defeating exercise, since they would make him so drowsy he was not much good when we arrived at the site. So he bravely discarded the comfort of the medication and with clenched teeth boarded one flight after another. Some help seemed to be had in the diversionary tactic of eating while aloft. So large bags of potato chips helped him avoid the need for other bags familiar to airplane passengers.

While the dreamer quality is there in Dan, the balance is practicality. One gets the impression that he likes to shock people with his ideas and present far-out concepts, then allow them to simmer, and wait for the returns in ideas they will accept and which are workable. Dan looks ahead constantly at possibilities and tries to guess what is coming. In this he is a futurist of the positive-thinking Christian variety.

Willing to let others stand in the spotlight, he works hard to provide them a stage and seems happiest when working behind the scenes to see that things operate the way they should. He is not jealous of others who might take his ideas as long as they are helping people.

Do you get the impression that Dan is a superhuman? He

is not. Just like the rest of us, he gets discouraged when the equipment malfunctions, materials are in short supply, and help is lacking. He just believes God wants the people in the next village to have a chance to hear the gospel in a form they can understand. To this end he has committed his talents and treasures to Christ.

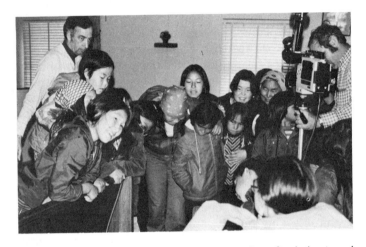

Eskimo youth watching themselves on the monitor after being taped for a "Northern Light" production in their village. Dr. Dan Etulain, far right; Pastor Van Dyne, standing, left.

9
Opportunities and Obstacles

Even play is hard work in Alaska. Nothing seems to come easily in this wilderness environment. Our family had an affinity for the out-of-doors. In Sitka this meant extensive preparation each time we ventured forth for work or play. Because of the predominately cold, rainy weather and the rugged terrain, hiking in the mountains was never a Sunday afternoon stroll through the park. It meant warm clothes, heavy boots, parkas, rain gear, emergency survival equipment, and telling someone where you were headed and when to expect you back.

Shortly after our arrival we developed a love for the ocean. This meant some kind of boat, life jackets, charts, and of course some fishing gear. There was the added danger of getting stranded on some isolated beach with no means of communication. Of course there was the dreaded but seldom talked about fear of being lost at sea or swamped by some freak wave or sudden storm and never being heard from again. Such dangers had to be faced and accepted before one could venture out of the relative safety of house or office.

So it was to be in this new ministry called ACTS-TV to which God was evidently calling us as a pastor and congregation—at least some members of the congregation who felt this was to be their special work. From the very beginning there were seemingly insurmountable obstacles. It seemed impossible that we could do anything about sharing the Good News in any form with people in small, isolated villages of another culture and another language.

In the summer of 1976 a letter from one of the "adopted" Eskimo girls in our family had brought home to me in a haunting way both the need to do something and the feeling of helplessness in the face of that need.

Liz Cleveland was one of the most beautiful, petite, shy, quiet Eskimo girls we had known. She came to be a part of our family when she was a freshman at Mount Edgecumbe. Two other girls made up our "adopted" family that year. At first we were convinced that Liz didn't understand our English. When we would try to talk to her, she said nothing. The other girls answered questions for her. So we just continued to make her welcome in our home and loved her.

During a city-wide crusade in Sitka with Bill Glass, Liz came forward to pray and accepted Christ as her Savior. It was a quiet conversion. After this she opened up and talked a little to us. But during that whole year we had more of a silent relationship with Liz than a verbal one. Her smile was enough reward for all we might have invested in her.

She did not return the next year to Sitka for school. Her parents convinced her that she was needed at home. So her education was interrupted. This was not unusual. We missed her and wrote to keep in touch. Then one day we received a letter which erased any doubt in my mind about the necessity of doing something about reaching out with God's love to the villages. Liz wrote:

Dear Pastor,

I need help. I want you to pray for my parents. You see—they have a drinking problem. They had it for years. I have been praying for them for two and a half years to turn their hearts to God, but I gave up. I know you don't want me to give up. I also prayed for myself. I want you, your family, and the Christian people of the Nazarene church to pray for us who are lost in sin, PLEASE! Right now my dad is drunk. 10:15 P.M. and I'm in tears. I am mad at the man who invited my dad to drink with him at his house.

Love,
Liz

P.S. Answer right away.

My heart was pierced. The village of Quinhagak where Liz lived was at least 1,200 miles away by small plane. I had no means to go. There was no Nazarene church within hundreds of miles of where she lived. What could I do? It was not until a week or two later that Mary Jo discovered written on the inside flap of the letter the word "HELP!"

Letters from other students came from time to time verifying the need for some kind of communication ministry that would allow Native Alaskan Christians to know about each other and to be nurtured in their faith in Christ. Dan Etulain received such a letter from a young man who had been a student of his at Sheldon Jackson College. He lived in a remote village of a few hundred people on the Yukon River where there was not a church of any kind.

Many students would come to Mount Edgecumbe High School for a year or two and then have to drop out because they were needed to help with family responsibilities back in the village. Consequently many of them were not able to finish their formal education on schedule if at all. The very first student we adopted in our family was with us only two years.

Ruth Martin was like Liz Cleveland. Her first means of communication with us was just to smile and say nothing. This changed when a young man in Sitka began to show an interest in her. She began to confide in me as a father about her feelings and frustrations with him. From then on we had verbal and written communication. English was definitely her second language. But this did not keep her from writing letters when she had to stay home to help care for her ailing mother. Here is an excerpt from one of her letters:

Hi! Thought I'd type up some word's while I got nothing to do here at the clinic. I'm so happy you send me the picture of the family. Wonder if I had send you the picture of mine, because I remember I was planning to send the picture of me. I can hardly think of what I did before Christmas. Because we were all so busy ready for Christmas. Please let me know if I isn't send a picture.

What I'm doing here at home is, I got a job as a community Health Aide. I really like the job. And it's the best job I've ever had compare to those other jobs I had. Also I'm gonna take Home College Courses like my sister is taking them. When I went to Bethel last Oct. for Health Aide Training, our Teacher helped me to take the College Course. Yet I got no High School Diploma. We had test and our Teacher told me that I can take the College Course. So starting from this month I'm gonna start my Home Course.

Well, we had a very enjoyable Christmas, and a New Year, but there was a missing guy from here, so the guys had to look for him. They found him, and he was fine. This Year theres been lot of missing guys, but they always find them.

This month were gonna have Song Feast here on 22 & 23, and also a Rally at Chefornak.

Well, I don'thave much to say now, but I think I'll see you all sometime in May if I go to my Brother's graduation. That is if God's will, and if Mom say's o-k if I ask her that I want to go. Got to go now till next time see you in letter and May God Bless.

Love,
Ruth Martin

P.S. Tell Nazarene Church People's I said Hello to them all.

So her English is not the best. (You should see my Yupik [you-pick]. On second thought, forget it.)

No doubt about it, the open door of need was set before us. But just as in setting out to climb a mountain behind our house in Sitka, it was going to be rough going in some spots. No decision to follow the call of God seems to be without some things which stand in the way of fulfillment of that call. I have not been able to subscribe to the theory that if we are in the will of God, all the lights will be green from here to the end of the goal. Maybe that works for some; it has not been true in my life. I have learned to take the obstacles with the opportunities.

Those obstacles came in a variety of ways. Almost at the exact time as the decision was made in my study that rainy night in the fall of 1977, a very attractive call was extended to us to return to southern California as a staff person in a large Nazarene church. It took several weeks to come to a point of decision about that. October was again one of the rainiest months of the year. An inch of rain a day gave us a feeling of kinship with Noah. Thoughts of southern sunshine were difficult to dismiss in such weather.

It seemed strange that we would even feel like turning down such an attractive offer when we had sought an easier and better place for so much of our ministry. Here was an offer to have relief from some of the less desirable duties of the pastorate; to have some degree of release from financial problems in the church; to have a house of our own; to live in an affluent society. The alternative to this was to live in an area of the world where we had to work hard physically just to exist; where the conveniences and luxuries of southern California were far from us; where the unknown would prove to be dangerous and difficult; where we were far from

59

loved ones; isolated from the world by water and distance; limited in travel possibilities; and on and on.

Yet I found myself leaning toward the challenge of the frontier and unknown rather than the security of a staff position.

On December 20 I wrote more of my thoughts to the Lord:

> When I look about me here there is little to offer me security or future success. Only a terrific need to preach the gospel to some who have never clearly heard about Jesus. There is little hope of financial return on the investment of our lives here. The people to whom we have been sent (Eskimo and Indian) are often poor in material goods compared to the people who live in southern California.

To remain in Alaska was to remain in semi-isolation from some of the things we held dear in our hearts—family; opportunity for better education for our children; material security; wider opportunities for advancement and ministry; variety of living experiences.

I took my cue from the words of Matt. 2:13—"Stay there until I tell you to return" (TLB). I was willing to wait for God's time for us to leave Alaska. I determined to work diligently until He called me elsewhere.

Apologies to all southern Californians. The Lord knows you need pastors there in great number. It was just the carrot being held in front of me at the time.

So we donned our parkas, our heavy boots, our backpacks, gathered our survival gear, and announced that we were going to "climb the mountain."

10
Across the Rolling Tundra

On the wall of my study was a large map of Alaska. When I first came the names on the map were foreign sounding to me. Now they were beginning to have a familiar ring. They felt like home territory more and more.

My attention was focused on the area between Bethel and Kuskokwim Bay. To that area of Alaska I hoped to go soon with an ACTS-TV television crew. It would be a journey into a great unknown, as much like going into the heart of a foreign country as any place in the world would be to me. Yet it was within the state of Alaska, my home state. I journaled:

> Lord, I trust You to go the way before me to these places. I do not want to be guilty of going in order to build up my ego or lift up myself. Help me to really lift up Jesus to the people I meet there. They need to see Him. Let there be open hearts to us as we visit a half dozen or so communities of Native Alaskan Eskimos.

Our goal was to see some of the high school students who made Sitka their home during the school year and came to our church. We prayed for the Lord to expand our vision of this group of people, to help us not to be guilty of exploiting them, but of loving them with the love of Jesus.

As I contemplated this journey to the villages I prayed: "Father, keep me growing to meet the challenge of these new assignments. Save me from stagnating at any one place in my journey through life. When I am of no more use here, then take me home with You."

One of the totems in Totem Park, a national monument in Sitka. The totems are literally family trees. They tell the story of the past through the use of symbols, depicting the various clans and some of the significant events. Contrary to the popular expression, the top man on the totem pole is the latecomer and consequently the least significant from the totem point of view.

I was beginning to understand more and more what God was talking about back there on that wind-blown hillside in Kansas when, as a boy, I heard Him speak to my heart of going to distant places to preach the gospel. Then the feeling was that it would be some exotic and foreign-speaking people, not to people in this very country. Then I had no thoughts of cold, remote, harsh, hostile Alaska.

Plans were made for an exploratory trip to the villages with our pilot television programs. We wanted to get some firsthand feedback from the people who were the object of our video production efforts. To keep expenses at a minimum we tied this trip in with the district assembly in Anchorage.

When she heard we were coming to her village of Quinhagak, Mary Oldfriend, one of the first Mount Edgecumbe students we met our first year in Sitka, wrote asking me, "Do you do weddings?" I wrote back assuring her that I did indeed "do weddings" but only if her local Moravian pastor would agree to assist.

The trip began immediately after the 1978 Alaska District Assembly. With Dr. Dan Etulain and Mr. Rod Nutting I boarded a Wein Air 737 jet for the flight to Bethel. It was a full plane. The front half of the jet was filled with cargo "igloos," and the rear half with people seated in non-leg-room-type seating. I was fortunate to have one of the front seats next to the wall dividing the passenger compartment from the cargo section. Wein Airline (at that time) did not have the extras other airlines use to lure passengers. It was a bare bones line. The flight attendant gave minimal service—no meals, just peanuts and 7-Up.

My seat neighbor was a young pastor from Kentucky who had been assigned to Bethel to start a church for another denomination. He had been there for about a year and had already been back to Anchorage nine times. Some of the experiences he shared about trying to get into the villages around Bethel were not too encouraging. He had been completely ignored and stranded several times. Still, I felt we would be well received since we were going to places where we knew students, and I *did* have an invitation to assist in a wedding in Quinhagak.

After flying over mountains and clouds, we descended to the plains of Bethel and the Kuskokwim River area. It impressed me as being rather like western Kansas. The difference was that there were thousands of small lakes dotting the surface of the land for as far as we could see. I learned that this is what the topography is like for hundreds of miles around—flat, treeless, and soggy. The only possible means of transportation in the summer is by riverboat or bush plane.

The Bethel airport was the epitome of basic necessities. In fact, some of those were missing. *Functional* would be the best word to describe all the facilities we would be seeing and using for the next six days.

We were met at the airport by Rick Myers, a white Anglo member of the local Moravian church. He worked for Wein as a supervisor of local operations. Rick enjoyed living in this community and filled us in on all the local happenings of interest. He and his wife, Sally, proved to be a most congenial host and hostess as we made their home our headquarters during our village visits.

After a rather long time we loaded our gear into Rick's van and rode into the town of Bethel where we stayed in the new house the Myers family was finishing while living in it. It was a comfortable dwelling complete with a "honey bucket" in the bathroom. We learned a new way to spell relief. There would not be the luxury of a flush toilet all the time we were in the area. This house did have running water and a shower in the bathroom. Extreme cold in the winter makes it economically impossible for there to be a city water and sewer system. Water is hauled to each house and stored in a large tank inside the house. The problem is not one of supply but of distribution. (This reminded me that there are other situations in our world where there is a problem of distribution.)

With our bags safely inside the Myers' house and having enjoyed a pleasant repast of crackers, dried oysters, and like delicacies we excused ourselves for a walk about town.

A light rain was falling and it was cool as we walked along one of the main roads (unpaved) of the village. We met several young people who recognized Rod from their associations at Mount Edgecumbe. It was good to see them and to receive a warm reception here on their home turf. We had not gone more than two blocks when a van screeched to a halt in front of us, and two young ladies came out calling to "Mr. Nutting." One of them, it turned out, worked for a local air charter line and recommended we fly with them. We walked on a few hundred feet and another van stopped. This time it was a pilot for Samuelson Air, the same flying service Louise had just recommended. We said we'd see about the possibility of using them in the morning to fly to our first village appointment.

We made one other contact that night, then headed back to the comfort of the house to go to bed on foam mattresses on the floor. We found them quite comfortable and soon drifted off to sleep.

Tuntatuliak

Samuelson Air got our business the first day. Squeezed into the confines of a Cessna 170 with our heavy baggage, we flew with Dave (6 months out of flight school in Florida) to the downriver community where we were to make our first attempt at sharing our TV pilot program of "The Northern Light." We planned to visit students and their families we had become acquainted with in Sitka, show them the video, and try to get some videotape of the people there singing and testifying.

The landing strip at Tuntatuliak was muddy, narrow, and

short. Rain was falling when we arrived. No one was there to meet us, so we started walking in the direction of the village, not at all sure if we would find a friendly welcome.

Shortly we saw the dark figure of a man running toward us. He turned out to be the Moravian church lay pastor, Phillip Charlie, coming to meet us. He spoke to us in broken English and Yupik. Soon others joined him. Among them were some of his children and some other students we knew. It was a pleasant greeting committee. They all accompanied us to the Charlie home.

The offer of coffee or tea was not long in coming. We accepted and were served a mixture of Lipton's tea and some Eskimo tea made from wild plants which grew on the tundra, delicious and mild. I drank several cups. The small children in the house became my friends when I tried the tactic of shaking hands with a piece of bubble gum or candy in my palm. We stayed for quite a while visiting with the children of the Charlie family who spoke very understandable English. Pastor Charlie was anxious to show us his crafts and skills and readily demonstrated them. The Eskimos are delightful people, and we came to love them very much.

When we expressed a desire to see the church building, we were led by boardwalk, to keep us from sinking into the thawing tundra, up a slight rise to the Moravian church. It was a simple structure. We were to find such churches in all the villages we visited. Inside were plain pews and a plain pulpit with a cross on the wall behind it. There was an old pump organ. I sat down and played some. It was a novel experience. Out the window the wind was gently blowing the wild artic cotton and short tundra grass. It reminded me so much of a Kansas rural schoolhouse or church building. A black oil-burning stove stood in the center of the one-room church with a pipe going through the ceiling above.

As we walked from the church to the school building, I visited with Pastor Phillip Charlie and made arrangements to set up our equipment to show the video. Soon a crowd gathered, summoned by CB radio. Everyone had one. There was a constant "party line" chatter going on all the time—most of it in Yupik.

On the way to the schoolhouse, I stopped to talk to a group of children who were creating pictures, using table knives to trace simple line drawings in the mud beside the boardwalk. Upon my offer to furnish candy, they eagerly drew more pictures, explaining them to me with happy excitement—in the Eskimo dialect. I enjoyed it immensely and understood not a word. I graciously declined what I took to be their invitation to demonstrate my artistic (?) ability.

The spirit of this group of children was contagious. When I stood up to go they followed me into the schoolhouse and hung around shyly to watch the proceedings. I could not help but fall in love with them. Even though they had almost nothing by "outside" standards, they appeared to be happy and loved. Life there seemed very stark and bleak to me, but in such situations little joys mean a lot.

The television presentation was well received. Phillip Charlie made a running commentary in Yupik and occasionally brought the house down with laughter at his comments, which we understood as clear as mud. Other times he yawned audibly. It was better than the Nielsen Rating System.

The time came for us to turn the lights on them and the camera toward their faces. The Eskimos were a willing group of TV stars. They sang loudly and beautifully.

The time passed too quickly and our plane was heard buzzing the village to pick us up for the return trip to Bethel for the night. We made a few quick visits in some of the homes of some of the students we knew. They offered and we accepted an Eskimo dessert called "agooduk" (agoo-duck), known in English as "Eskimo ice cream." It is an uncooked dessert made by mixing Crisco or seal oil with generous portions of sugar and wild berries. Entering an Eskimo home is a little different from entering a typical white Anglo residence. We knocked and entered after a voice from within said, "Come in." Meeting your guests at the door is not customary, and doors are seldom locked.

Rooms in an Eskimo home are often multipurpose. Housing is built under difficult circumstances. Materials are hard and expensive to come by. So the central room often serves as kitchen-living-dining-family room. Some homes consist of a single room for sleeping, eating, and visiting. The lack of privacy takes some getting used to by us gussicks. If there was a lack of luxuries, it was soon forgotten in the presence of an abundance of hospitality.

Our departure could be delayed no longer, so we hurried to the airport, accompanied by several people who were happy to help us with our baggage.

"First village: very good reception and experience."

Quinhagak (quinn-a-hawk)

Liz Cleveland and Mary Oldfriend lived here. Liz was still the shy, beautiful teenager we had known in Sitka. She followed us around the village and spoke gratefully of our having come to her hometown.

Quinhagak sits on a dull grey and treeless land where the Kuskokwim (Kus-ko-quim) River empties into the North Pacific. A cold wind kept our outside excursions to a minimum. Since it was our 21st wedding anniversary I wanted to call home to talk to Mary Jo. I was told there was one phone in the village. When I located it in the city hall, I realized this would not exactly be a private conversation. With 30 Eskimos standing around I conveyed my love across the miles to my wife.

Here our schedule was even busier than at Tuntatuliak. We arrived early in the morning, counseled with the bride and groom, had an afternoon wedding, attended the

68

Wednesday night meeting in the Moravian church, and showed our video program. Following that we stayed up past midnight videotaping this beautiful group of people singing and sharing their testimonies.

The wedding of Mary Oldfriend to John Hill was a bilingual, cross-cultural event. The Moravian pastor and I shared the ceremony. One of the nontraditional aspects was the announcement in Yupik of the showing of "The Northern Light" television show after the Wednesday night prayer meeting.

So in the little white clapboard church by the eroding

Dora Roberts, one of the Van Dynes' "adopted" children, with her mother and little sister in the church at Quinhagak.

riverbank in Quinhagak, Alaska, wedding vows were ex-changed while a jam-packed room full of family and friends smiled their approval. After her wedding, Mary returned to take part in the TV taping session.

The wedding of John and Mary (Oldfriend) Hill in Quinhagak

I think Mary would be an excellent television performer for ACTS-TV. She has a naturally beautiful voice and plays the guitar better than most. Above all, she wants to share Jesus.

I missed a once-in-a-lifetime opportunity to take a bath in an Eskimo sweat house with the village men. I'm not sure I'll ever forgive Dan for keeping that videotaping session go-ing so late. It would have felt so good on a near-freezing drizzling night before going to bed in the upstairs room of the Moravian parsonage.

Because of the distance we stayed overnight in Quin-hagak and had the chartered bush plane and pilot pick us up the next morning for a flight to the next village on our agenda.

Kipnuk (Kip-nook)

The inexperience of our six-months-out-of-flight-school pilot became evident as we were making our way from Quinhagak to Kipnuk. The weather was hazy. With the nondescript landscape below, landmarks were hard to come by. I knew we were not exactly with a veteran pilot when he handed the chart to me and said, "See if you can find that river."

Now I'm a pilot of a few hundred hours experience flying in California so I knew how to read a chart and what landmarks look like from the air, but so help me, I never could find that river. By some hook or crook we managed to find the landing strip at Kipnuk and touched down on what looked more like a river than a landing strip. The pilot had to scrape the mud off the wings before taking off.

As at Tuntatuliak, no one was at the airstrip to meet us. We found our way the short distance to the cluster of houses which are barely above high tide. We were not long in finding the home of Ruth Martin, our first "adopted" daughter. What a joy it was to meet her family and find such a warm, loving reception! Even though her parents had little if any understanding of our language and we none of theirs, our spirits were knit together in the bond of God's love.

The church building was the scene for our TV act. Even though it was the height of the fishing season and many families were at temporary fishing camps up the river, the church building was filled to capacity at two o'clock on a Tuesday afternoon. Never have we had a more appreciative audience nor a more prepared group to perform than we found in that Moravian church building on the treeless, trackless coast of southwest Alaska.

The time we stayed in Kipnuk was cut short with the sound of our plane overhead. It was heart-wrenching to have to leave Ruth and her family and friends. When would we ever be able to return?

Akiak (Ack-ee-ack)

During our overnight stay in Bethel after leaving Kip-nuk, we had a conference with the local Moravian pastor since we had heard there was to be a funeral in Akiak the day we had scheduled to be there. We were reluctant to barge in with television equipment when the community would be in mourning. But the pastor encouraged us to go ahead. So with some hesitancy we flew the next day upriver to what has got to be the "mosquito capital of the world."

One of the unusual sights we saw here was a nearly new car. The unusual thing about that was the fact that there were no roads leading out of this tiny village. When we inquired as to the use for this vehicle we were told it was for driving to Bethel in the winter. You see, the Kuskokwim River freezes over and makes a perfectly good highway—until the spring thaw, of course.

News of our arrival spread quickly by CB and word of mouth. Soon we were being invited into various homes for coffee and tea. Old acquaintances with former students were renewed. We visited with the young lay pastor about the funeral and about our interest in getting a feel from the people for ACTS-TV. He assured us they wanted to go ahead with our appearance after the funeral was over.

The events that followed are stamped permanently in my heart and mind.

Last Rites for Katie Ivan

The little tin-roofed church building was far too small for the crowd trying to get inside. When we arrived after visiting with the young Eskimo pastor-fisherman next door, there was standing room only. All the wooden benches which served for pews were filled to overflowing, so we found a place to stand near the wall for the hour-and-a-half service.

The sanctuary was plain by any standard. Dominated by

72

an oil-burning stove in the center of the room, it was orna-mented with a wooden cross backed by a purple curtain. An ancient pump organ provided accompaniment for the sing-ing. The pulpit was a simple wooden lectern in the middle of the slightly raised platform.

Since the service was in the Yupik Eskimo dialect I could not understand the words. But the spirit of the singing and the mood of the people could not be disguised behind the barrier of language.

There was no funeral director, no ushers, no finely robed minister, no pungent fragrance of cut flowers beautifully ar-ranged. Only the hushed cry of babies and the whispered greetings from sorrowing faces beneath the summer parkas filled the musty atmosphere of a room too full of people.

The influence of 100 years of Moravian missions was evident in the simple service. Four pastor-fishermen dressed in clean blue jeans and work shirts were present to give mes-sages in the Eskimo language understood by all except these strangers with the pale white faces.

In their quiet, beautiful way these descendants of the oldest Americans welcomed us as honored guests. They al-lowed us to be in attendance at the homegoing celebration for Katie Ivan.

The coffin was a simple, homemade wooden box cov-ered with white sheets inside and out. In it lay the tiny body of "Aunt Katie," as many people had lovingly called her. She was wrapped in a white sheet. A small bouquet of faded plastic flowers had been placed on her bosom.

Choirs and quartets from surrounding villages sang songs about heaven and the end of sufferings here on earth. Beautiful harmony filled the heavy damp air inside the church. Sung slowly and sincerely, these old hymns echoed the poignant emotions of a people long used to survival in the harsh tundra land of Alaska. The realities of life and death are thinly disguised here. Still, there was a dignity and beauty about this gathering which I would not have traded for a memorial service in the grandest cathedral on earth.

When the last sermon had been given and the last choir had sung, the old pump organ began to give forth the strains of "Sweet By-and-bye" as the congregation sang softly in the language of Eskimos the same song sung by Christians the world around.

At the singing of this hymn about heaven, the people filed forward past the plain, simple box to pay their respects to this little Eskimo woman who had been blind all her 60 years. She often expressed the hope during her lifetime of being able to see Jesus when she got to heaven.

They came first from outside the building where they had waited patiently all during the service. Altogether, nearly 300 walked past the coffin as the organ continued its labored playing and the soft melody of the hymn was punctuated with the tolling of the bell atop a wooden tower by the church door.

Finally, when all had viewed the body for the last time, one of the pastors stepped to the side of the platform where a white, cloth-covered piece of plywood was propped against the wall. The sound of hammer and nails filled the building as he fastened the cover on the coffin before the silent congregation in a ceremony of primitive eloquence signifying the finality of death.

We followed the family and friends of "Aunt Katie" outside to the plot of ground nearby reserved for burial. Following a few appropriate words and a prayer, the young pastor-fisherman shoveled the first dirt onto the coffin. Others joined in the necessary work to cover the box. The watching mourners were bathed in the coolness of a gentle summer rain. The birds were singing. Katie Ivan was home.

Several years have passed since that summer day of 1978 in Akiak. Whenever I think of it, emotions difficult to express rise up within me. Never have I felt so honored, so helpless, so blessed, so empty, and so full at the same time as when I was privileged to see into the hearts of Alaska's lovely, though too often misunderstood and forgotten people who have learned to live with the ebb and flow of nature, time, and the Creator who gives life and receives it back again.

Akiachuk (Ack-ee-ah-chuck)

One other village, Akiachuk, was visited on this first ACTS-TV trip to the villages. It was no exception in giving us a warm welcome. They too were excited about the possibilities we shared of using video as a communication tool for them to speak and sing to each other.

Returning home to Sitka, we realized we had certainly taken on more than we could handle with our limited resources and skill. Once again I realized that if anything was going to be done in the villages, God would have to do it; I certainly was not capable.

There was no time for review upon my return home from the district assembly and the extended trip we had taken into the villages. I was plunged immediately into a busy schedule with a growing congregation which demanded my time and attention in the immediate vicinity of Sitka. ACTS-TV and its development would have to take a backseat for a while.

11
People from Remotest Lands

Most of us live our lives from one sunrise or sunset to another. But then, most of us do not live beyond the Arctic Circle. Those who live there have a different set of days. It is difficult to describe what an arctic day or night is like to someone who has never experienced one. They are special creations—like rubber bands, they have an elastic quality making them capable of stretching and contracting.

Half the year is filled with light-spun days when there is hardly any sunset—just constant light. In fact there are many days in the middle of the summer when the sun never drops below the horizon. The other half of the year is made of days when the rays of the sun are gold in value as well as color. Then the sun sets to be seen no more above the horizon for long winter night-days.

It was in this land beyond the sunset that a bright young man lived who brought much cheer to the inhabitants of a tiny village called Kivalina. He was born in the middle of a loving family where the old Eskimo ways were lived out as the normal way of life. Those ways were soon to change with the dawning of a new day brought on by the discovery of oil even farther north in the Prudhoe Bay "north slope" field. But life "beyond the sunset" was going to change even more with the coming of this bouncing baby boy and the coming again of the summer sun.

I tell you this story because Roger Adams's life and death became the catalyst which got ACTS-TV moving.

It begins in the summer of 1974, the same summer we arrived in Sitka from Santa Barbara to begin our pastorate. I met Roger at the corner of Lincoln and Halibut Point Road. A staff member of Sheldon Jackson College introduced us. He was one of the most unusual Eskimos I ever met. Outspoken, boisterous, sometimes very noisy, he laughed easily and loved to joke in the Eskimo way. The man who introduced me to this lively Eskimo said, "Watch that young Eskimo; he's going far." And over the course of the four years he lived after that I had many occasions to observe him at close range. Now I wish with all my heart I had paid closer attention. Strange, isn't it, how we often miss the best things in life because we think we are too busy when they come to us in unexciting moments on common, ordinary days.

But I really couldn't help but stop once in a while to listen to and watch this bouncing Eskimo. He was like—a bouncing basketball. He loved the game. Really couldn't play well. His small stature was against him. But you didn't dare tell that to Roger. It was like trying to shout down the noise of a jet taking off. Most of the time in official games he was playing from the bench. But the bench never had a livelier participant in the game. He refused to be put down if he couldn't play.

When he first came to college, his zeal for the Lord was sometimes like a basketball too—up and down. He would break the rules and yield to the temptations of the "big-city life in Sitka" by getting drunk. But the next morning he would be in the dean's office confessing his misdeeds to Prof.

Darrell Moore, asking forgiveness and another chance to prove himself.

But a spiritual change took place in Roger's life, and he began to sense God's call to preach. I shall not forget one Sunday night in a testimony service in the Nazarene church hearing Roger tell the congregation, "I must go back to my village and tell them about Jesus." The burden for his own people was so intense that he was convinced he should quit school and go immediately. We counseled him to stay and finish school. He was so close to graduating. He finally went back, but it was in a coffin.

Death came to Roger while he was playing a basketball game. An autopsy revealed a brain aneurysm which had been there from birth as the cause of death. Perhaps he had a premonition that the end was near when he spoke of needing to go back immediately.

Death came to him in the springtime. That is when we met Ruth and Caleb Adams, Roger's parents. They came to Sitka for the memorial service there. They were typical Eskimo in looks, dress, and language—lovely people. Mary Jo and I fell in love with them at first sight. Even though the family was Episcopal in church membership and the Alaskan Episcopal bishop was in Sitka, I was asked to conduct a portion of the funeral in the college chapel.

Roger Adams was born beyond the sunset. He was buried beyond the sunset. His life influence extended far beyond the sunset.

Upon our return from that first visit to the villages in the Bethel area, Dan Etulain began to talk about making a television special about Roger's life and influence. He thought we would need to go to his home and spend time with his parents to really tell the story right. We made it a matter of prayer.

Six months after his death, I found myself walking across the airstrip at Kivalina in the soft twilight of an October winter's evening. I spent several days in the village where he grew to manhood, the village where he finally was laid to rest in the cemetery next to the runway. From his gravesite there is an unobstructed view of the sun setting across the Bering Sea.

The decision to go to Kivalina was made after an invitation was extended to us to visit the Adams family. This required extensive preparation and loads of equipment. Somehow we convinced Alaska Airlines to carry our 16 pieces of luggage for no extra charge. Travel in Alaska demands more than the usual number of bags, especially when you are going to be recording video in a place where there is no dependable electrical power.

Our crew for this major production included Dave Kimbrough, an administrative officer in the U.S. Forest Service and a member of Sitka Church of the Nazarene. He along with Dan Etulain and I lived for a few days with the Adamses.

Our all-volunteer, unpaid staff was increased by one when we arrived at the site with the pilot of our chartered MARC Cessna Skymaster. MARC (Missionary Aviation and Repair Center) out of Soldotna, Alaska, is run by dedicated self-supported missionaries who, when time and distance require, will stay with their client and join in their work. They are greatly used by churches in the villages and by missionary agencies in Alaska for transportation. Cost is limited to little more than fuel. We never could have afforded to charter a commercial bush plane for that distance.

So on an October day, Dave, Dan, and I boarded Alaska Airlines regular flight to Anchorage where we met our MARC pilot. After an overnight stay with Mike and Vonnie Stone, former Sitka Nazarenes, we set out through the mountain passes and across the rolling tundra for hours of flying. After a refueling stop in Kotzebue (Kot-see-boo) we flew another hour or more to Kivalina (Kiv-ah-lean-ah).

Kivalina is a place you really have to see to believe it even exists. It is located just a few feet above high tide on a teardrop-shaped spit of land. In fact at high tide the village becomes an island. The waves of the Bering Sea sweep over the narrow string of land connecting it with the mainland of that part of Alaska which is mostly "inhabited" by the formidable Brooks Mountain Range.

From the air it gives the appearance of an Eskimo yo-yo. It looks like a tiny ball of sealskin stuffed with people, swung on the end of a slender string of seal gut.

Here at the mercy of all the elements of nature in the far north, a community of rugged people has existed for thousands of years—fighting against the tide, or perhaps more accurately, living in harmony with it. There was literally nothing between them and all that arctic weather can dish out. They are so far north that Siberia is south.

The land on which a variety of houses and public buildings stand is only a few hundred yards long and not as wide. It shelters a lagoon where the waters of a river and the incoming tide meet.

The World War II remnant of a metal landing strip embedded in the sand is nearly as wide as the thread of land on which it is laid out.

A new school building dominates this village of a few hundred residents. There is the usual village store. The high cost of transporting groceries is evident in the prices—eggs for $3.00 a dozen, when you can get them.

Two churches, Friends and Episcopal, offer the people of Kivalina spiritual strength. They coordinate their Sunday evening services so one can attend both. The necessary bell for calling the congregation to services stands atop a rustic wooden tower beside these cathedrals of the north. Like most everything else in this barren land, they are more functional than beautiful.

The school building is multipurpose. It houses offices,

classrooms, a gymnasium-cafeteria, and is the gathering place for any large community meeting. Standing on stilts to protect the permafrost (keep the ground from thawing out from the heat radiated by the building), it has the appearance of a square spaceship which has just landed. Nevertheless, it is a vital part of the place, being the principal employer and the educator of the populace.

Life here seems to center around the school, the store, and the churches. Although computers are a classroom tool, children are entertained by simpler things than the complicated gadgets of most of Western society. They find great fun in sliding on the ice in the lagoon and beachcombing for driftwood along the edge of the sea.

The hunt is still a part of the life-style for these descendants of the first inhabitants of this part of the world. It may take the form of stalking seals and walruses on the icy waters of the ocean or pursuing the land game of caribou and reindeer. Nothing is taken except to supply food for the family. Even so there is a respect for the life which is given so the Eskimos may eat. Usually a piece of the slain animal is thrown back into the sea or left on the land as a symbolic way of saying thanks to the animal for giving its life so they might have food.

Young Eskimo boys who show the interest are taught to hunt almost as soon as they can walk. They are taken along on the hunts and shown more than told how to bring home the necessary food.

In the summer there are salmonberries, blueberries, and low bush cranberries to pick. Small game and waterfowl help supplement the diet of things bought at the general store.

The women of the village are adept at sewing parkas and kuspics (a summer parka made of cotton designed as a pullover reaching to just above the knees and worn with another dress or pants). Many have electric sewing machines. Other modern conveniences appear as money is available and

81

electric power can be obtained from the community oil-burning generator.

Like hundreds of other Alaskan rural villages, there is a schedule revolving around the coming of the mail planes. These pilots and their planes fly the invisible threads which connect village with village. They bring hope and good news, when the weather permits them to fly. Their absence adds to the darkness of spirit which can descend upon a body in the dead of winter. They can literally spell the difference between life and death to the people in Kivalina and other villages. (A one-year-old granddaughter of Ruth and Caleb Adams died of pneumonia shortly after we were there because the weather made it impossible for her to be flown 70 miles to Kotzebue for medical aid which could have saved her life.)

The approach of a small plane overhead turns the focus of everyone's attention to the runway which stops short of the houses in town. Winter or summer, it makes no difference, the standard vehicle to meet these incoming planes is a "sno-go" (otherwise known as a snowmobile) pulling a wooden dogsled. It doesn't matter that there is no snow in the summer or early fall—the sno-go and sled operate just the same. Strange things are seen in the Land of the Midnight Sun.

Upon our arrival our baggage was loaded on the dogsled and pulled by the sno-go to the Adams igloo. Of course it wasn't an ice igloo—sorry to disappoint you, but those are only used when the men are on a hunt in the dead of winter. It was made of unpainted plywood. A single outside door led first into a sort of anteroom, then into the warm kitchen. It was definitely not a tract house in suburbia. But it was typical of those houses in Kivalina which have replaced the old sod, driftwood, and skin igloos of only a few years back.

The inside of the house was one of utilitarian disarray. A stove in the middle of the kitchen served to both heat and cook. A clothesline strung from one side of the room to the other demanded attention with its burden of towels, washcloths, and, on washday, the family wash. A plain wooden table with benches rather than chairs served as both a worktable and dining place. Bare electric light bulbs hung from wires protruding out of the ceiling. There were three bedrooms all packed full of beds, cots, and limited storage space. Curtains in the doorways sufficed for privacy.

Small on the outside, it was unlimited in room inside because there was an unmistakable atmosphere of love. No *Better Homes and Gardens* model, this house, but I have never been in a lovelier home.

In one corner of the largest room which served as kitchen-living-dining-wash room was a curtained-off area where one could enjoy the privacy of the "honey bucket" without having to interrupt a conversation with the hostess as she prepared bread for baking in the oven of the oil-burning stove.

There was evidence of poured-out love for the children who had blessed that home. A dusty row of trophies which Roger had won in high school and college days occupied a place of importance on some shelves on the wall near the dining table.

One of Roger's brothers met us at the plane and took us to the house. Since it had only been six months since Roger's untimely death in Sitka we were apprehensive about how Ruth Adams would feel about our coming to her home to talk about him and do some video recording for a special ACTS-TV presentation. Four gussicks barging into the house with loads of baggage might be too much of a shock, we thought.

Our fears were quickly allayed as shortly after we introduced ourselves all around, Mrs. Adams said in her broken English, "I pray." It was a simple announcement of what she was about to do. That kitchen-living-dining-wash room became an anteroom to heaven as she eloquently and emotionally, in her native Inupiak (In-new-pea-ack, the northern Eskimo dialect), poured out her soul to God. We did not understand a word, but there was no misunderstanding the spirit with which she prayed.

When she had finished we listened as she explained to us her own fears about our coming. She was not sure how she would feel, but now, "It's OK."

For four days we were guests in this humble home. And I do mean guests. We were treated like royalty and at the same time allowed to see into every facet of the Adams family life. Laughter and tears flowed freely as we remembered the joy-filled life of their middle son.

Ruth and Caleb allowed us to probe their feelings and memories for insights into this life which had had such an influence in a short time in so many places. We were given the privilege of talking for long periods of time in front of a TV camera with Ruth and Caleb.

As we walked about the village and talked with others who knew Roger, we discovered that he had been a lift to the spirits of young and old alike. In both church congregations there were people who told us stories of his bright spirit.

One of the fascinating things we came across while we were there was a group of 40 young people who returned from a 70-mile trip by chartered planes to the next village north and west of Kivalina—Point Hope. These youth had become concerned about their friends there who did not know Christ. At the expense of $2,600 of their own hard-earned money, they made the trip for the weekend to share in song and testimony their faith in Christ.

These young Eskimos graciously consented to give us a concert in the Friends church. I would be hard put to find such intensity of spiritual drive as motivated them. Now I understood something of the spirit of Roger when he had expressed the desire in our church in Sitka to return to his own village to tell them of Jesus.

On Sunday we attended both the Episcopal and Friends services. I was invited to speak in both the evening services. This was a highlight of my ministry. It had been a boyhood dream to someday visit the Antarctic. Here I was near the opposite end of the earth's axis experiencing the privilege of preaching the gospel to people of a different culture and a different language. When I came to the close of that day I felt like saying, "Lord, You can take me on home to heaven now; I have done it all!"

Why all this fuss over one Eskimo, you ask? We were convinced that the primary mission of ACTS-TV was to provide a tool for Native Americans to speak to each other about the love of God. Roger's life story could be an open door to make this possible. We did not want to paint him larger than life, if we could help it; we just wanted to show the Native community that there were real Christians in the villages of Alaska with whom they could identify. It was a first attempt. Would it work? This question was in our minds as we packed our gear in the MARC plane and headed down the narrow runway to start our journey home.

As we circled the village for the last time we saw a poignant reminder of Roger Adams's love for his native land and for the ancient Eskimo ways which were fast passing away. The pilot flew low over the site of an unfinished summer hunting igloo which Roger was working on the last time he was home. It was on the banks of a river a few miles from the present site of Kivalina. I wanted so much to walk up the narrow strip of land to the mainland, but the winter was not set in enough for us to traverse that path. I vowed someday to return in the summer and visit it.

We returned to Sitka to begin the tedious process of putting together the first ACTS-TV special with the prayer that we would be allowed to broadcast it on the state satellite system when it was in place. Several obstacles had to be overcome before we would see that dream realized. Producing

Christian television in Alaska with extremely limited equipment and even more limited skills was proving to be a nearly insurmountable obstacle.

Something that Ruth Adams said as we were leaving her house for the last time stuck in my mind and refused to let me forget why we were spending all this time and effort to communicate across the vast distances to small groups of people of a different culture. Trying to sum up what our coming and telling Roger's story meant to her, she said, "You have been like a Band-Aid to my heart!" I have never received, nor do I ever expect to receive, a higher compliment.

12
Give Me This Mountain

Mountain climbing became a vital part of our life-style in Sitka. We loved the mountains. They were so close we could reach out and touch them from just about anywhere we went.

I wanted to climb them all. Cheri and Peter shared that desire with me from the beginning. Mary Jo only shared it on rare occasions—but when she did she was right there alongside of the rest of the family, carrying her share of the load and digging her fingernails in for a better hold. (She joined us once on a five-day journey on the 35-mile Chilkoot Trail and carried 35 pounds on her back—one-third her weight.)

The peak closest to our house tantalized us with its nearness, and often I could hear it calling, especially on those rare and beautiful sun-filled summer days when it would be daylight until near midnight.

For seven years I climbed the mountain with Peter. He was only 11 when we first ascended the heights above Sitka the distance of one "verst" (a Russian mile). Even that first time he got to the top long before I did. The mountain's real name is Verstovia (Ver-stove-ee-ya).

Every morning I looked out the window of our house to

see if I could get a glimpse of the mountain. Often I could not see its peak. On those rare occasions when it was not shrouded in the mist and clouds, its outline was etched unforgettably against the sky. When we moved closer to the mountain I found myself even more fascinated by it.

Its base is at sea level. The trail begins in a thicket of salmonberry bushes. The path which climbs up its side is rugged and steep. Halfway up each time I vowed that it would be my last attempt. Every muscle and bone in my body ached in objection to the climb. My heart beat loudly in my ears.

Back and forth across the face of the mountain we climbed. Under fallen trees, over huge rocks, the path led us on. On the lower elevations tall spruce trees of a second growth reach for the sky where the first Russian settlers logged the mountainside for timber to build their forts and houses and for making charcoal to burn in their ships' galleys. The tops of these trees are in excess of 100 feet above the ground. Their roots have found a tenacious grasp in the thin soil covering the granite rocks.

I forced myself to take each step. Only the thought of the goal at the top in the clearing above the timberline kept me putting one foot tortuously in front of the other. Never have I been disappointed with the results of the climb. The sight at the top is spectacular.

From the outcropping of rocks which mark the highest point we enjoyed a panorama of rugged peaks, deep ocean inlets, snow-filled valleys, and tree-covered hills. Across the ocean channel the Fujiyama shape of the extinct volcano called Mount Edgecumbe stands etched against the vastness of the North Pacific which stretches to the horizon. Far, far below us we looked down on the "toy" town where we lived. How small it appeared! How small it was!

From the vantage point of the rock where we sat, our eyes feasted on the tantalizing peak of Mount Arrowhead, another hour's climb away. The trail to its summit was far more demanding and twice as enticing to us. We had climbed it before and knew its rigors as well as the reward of the breathtaking beauty for those who put it beneath their feet. My journal record of one climb says:

But today we must turn back. Duty calls from below, and we run down the mountain in half the time it takes us to climb up. The hour down is filled with resolve to climb again even though knee joints voice a hundred protests.

Now in this late July evening, I lift my eyes to the window and see the mountain beckoning me. I will resist for a while its verdant charms and rocky precipices, but not for long. Again and again I will succumb to the call of the mountain.

It speaks to me as an old and wise friend. "Nothing worth having is easy. The climb is hard and demanding of all that you can give, but the reward at the top is worth it all."

From up there I can look back down on the house where we live. I can get a better perspective on the place of my life and ministry.

Jesus often called His followers aside to the mountains for retreat and renewal with the words, "Come apart . . . and rest a while." Many times I have answered that call by literally going up this and other mountains around here to get a better perspective on the events of my life.

Now the clouds are moving in again to cover the mountain with mist and mystery. It will disappear from my view, but I will always know it is there. I can go there in my spirit and mind whenever I choose.

"Lord, there are other mountains which I must climb to reach goals You have set before me. Help me to be as diligent in climbing them as I was today in climbing Verstovia.

"One thing more. Someday help me to climb the

89

mountain right on up to heaven. In the meantime, keep me climbing for as long as You want here below. Help me to not be afraid to run back down from the mountain of inspiration to the sea level village of responsibility and ministry. There is much to be done here.

"Thanks for the mountains."

There was a healing, mind-clearing therapy about mountain climbing for me. Once when I was struggling with a call to return to a church "outside" as pastor, Cheri sensed my stress and said to me, "Dad, I think it's time you climbed another mountain."

The mountaintop of getting ACTS-TV programming on the air beckoned. We could no longer ignore it. So we started out.

Climbing this first peak of actually getting a program on the state satellite system meant long hours late at night, after we had all finished our regular job assignments, putting the pieces of the program together from all the taping we had done in the various villages and especially in Kivalina.

Getting through the underbrush of learning how to actually edit programs without any formal training and with very limited equipment was sometimes discouraging. Learning to work together so we would all get to the top of the mountain together was sometimes a chore in itself. We felt God molding us into a team.

Of course the demands of pastoring a growing church for me, of being a full-time college professor for Dan, and a full-time administrator for the Forest Service for Dave left little time for what amounted to a full-time task just to try to produce a program a month. Our naive ambition at the beginning of the project had been to produce a 30-minute program a week. It was to take us six months just to put the Roger Adams story together. Our supply of midnight oil ran low.

Necessity often helps us to find shortcuts. God put in our

path an opportunity which necessitated our making a Christmas program in just two weeks. It came about when we got the brilliant idea of taping the annual appearance of the Mount Edgecumbe High School choir at the local retirement center, the Alaska Pioneers Home.

We were told by the state administrators of the satellite television system that Alaska-generated Christmas specials were being sought.

This motivated us to give it a try. We received permission from the Pioneer Home administration to bring our camera to the concert. It turned out beautifully. We were able to make a good program. It included interviews with some of the Christian Alaska Pioneers who lived in the home.

Anxiously we waited for Christmas Eve of 1978 to see if they would really air it. Sure enough, right after the live broadcast from the governor's mansion in Juneau here came "The Northern Light" special, "Christmas at the Pioneer Home." We were elated. At last we were seeing a crack in the door to the villages.

We received phone calls from people in villages who saw the program. Praise God! We had made it to the top of the first peak.

This opened the door and we were able to air several "Northern Light" specials the following year, at no cost to the ministry. These programs were accepted because they were focused on Native Alaskans and contained historical and educational material.

Because of the more straightforward evangelical appeal of other programs they were not allowed to be aired. This was disappointing at first, but we took it to be the Lord's direction. Had we been allowed to air overtly evangelical religious programming, then other non-Christian religious groups would have demanded equal time and treatment.

Consequently programs aired over the state's system have this native/educational/historical flavor. But this has not kept Eskimos and Indians from sharing Christ through their music and comments in programs which are advertised to show Native Alaskan art and talent.

The director and part of the choir from Point Barrow at the annual Native New Life Musicale in Anchorage.

One of the opportunities which appeared on the horizon soon in the development of this ministry was an annual Native Musicale which takes place every January in Anchorage in the dead of winter.

The musicale is a gathering of Native Christians for two or three nights in a high school auditorium to sing gospel songs and old hymns in native languages as well as English. For two and a half hours an evening the auditorium is filled with up to 2,000 people listening to one group after another from across the state sing praises and share testimonies.

The various ethnic groups in Alaska have naturally been anxious to retain their special identity. But in these musical gatherings those barriers have been erased, and a spirit of oneness in Christ has prevailed. As these meetings have increased in popularity from year to year, ACTS-TV has been invited back to tape them for production of hour-long specials which have been accepted for satellite broadcast.

After six years of this kind of programming we began to see and hear tangible results of this means of communicating the gospel to the villages. Stories of encouragement from having seen familiar native faces on the television rather than just unfamiliar white faces, made worthwhile the effort it took to travel to Anchorage every February and spend the days and nights necessary to produce these programs.

An interesting sidelight for me at the very first Native Musicale I helped cover was the meeting of an Eskimo woman I had pastored years before in Hawaii. What wondrous ways God has of weaving the fabric of our lives together into a pattern we would never have thought of ourselves!

From the beginning we knew that ways would have to be found to make inspirational and Bible study tapes available to the individual in the villages as well as the "Northern Light" specials which were broadcast occasionally on the state-wide satellite television system.

Mrs. Hill, an Eskimo woman, and two of her grandchildren who live in Hooper Bay. She showed the author how to weave grass baskets.

One of the factors which made it possible for us to go to the villages was the support of the Alaska district superintendent, Rev. Robert Sheppard, and the entire district. ACTS-TV has been included in the district budget for a modest amount each year since 1978.

The need for native leadership to be trained to go back to the villages was recognized by the district leadership. When it became apparent that Alaska was too small a district to have its own Bible college and that sending Native Alaskans "outside" for college was not succeeding on a significant scale, the focus of reaching these scattered, isolated rural areas was turned to this fledgling ministry called ACTS-TV.

So the meaning of the letters widened to mean Alaska Christians Telling the Story To Villagers. While the production of video with and for Native Alaskans is still the central focus, it is apparent that related ways of reaching into the

94

villages will have to accompany the use of television. There will always be the need for frequent trips to the various villages to participate in church services and special meetings as well as for print media to make the videotapes more useful in training and Christian nurture.

13
Acts Chapter 29

Two of the New Testament writers had a definite sense of writing about something that was only beginning. (See Mark 1:1 and Acts 1:1.) Both end on an unfinished note. There is no doubt in my mind but that this was intentional.

The New Testament Book of Acts has no chapter 29. But I cannot argue that the Holy Spirit has stopped writing in the lives of Christians ever since that first Christian century. We are Acts 29!

This book will also end on an unfinished note. That is exactly because what is recorded here is only a little of the story of the beginning of something which will doubtless grow and expand as the Holy Spirit continues to burden the hearts of Christians to do something about those people who have yet to join the chorus of praise described in Psalm 67.

This scripture really became mine when I traveled to the village of Kivalina beyond the Arctic Circle:

> God be gracious to us and bless us,
> And cause His face to shine upon us—Selah.
> That Thy way may be known on the earth,
> Thy salvation among all nations.
> Let the peoples praise Thee, O God;

Let all the peoples praise Thee.
Let the nations be glad and sing for joy;
For Thou wilt judge the peoples with uprightness,
And guide the nations on the earth. Selah.
Let the peoples praise Thee, O God;
Let all the peoples praise Thee.
The earth has yielded its produce;
God, our God, blesses us.
God blesses us,
That all the ends of the earth may fear Him.

(NASB)

However, I must tell you a few things which are being written in chapter 29 about ACTS-TV. For while my physical location is not in Alaska at the writing of this book, my heart still holds this ministry in a special place. Involvement for me now includes telling others about this ministry and occasionally returning to Sitka and Anchorage to assist in special productions.

It was with a great deal of soul-searching that we finally decided to leave Alaska and accept a place of ministry in the "lower 48." At the time we didn't understand what God was doing in our lives. Now the purpose seems clearer. I have learned to trust the leadings of the Lord and know that in His time He truly does all things well. My business is to follow—in sunshine and rain.

But before we left we were able to see the arrival of the first full-time, self-supported missionary for ACTS-TV. Sybil Salisbury, a part Navajo Indian woman, came to us with a burden for Native Americans—her own people. Her church affiliation was with the Wesleyan Methodist church. During her time in Sitka she joined the Nazarene church. From the beginning she not only gave herself unreservedly to the many office duties for the ministry but went far beyond with a personal involvement in the lives of the students at Mount Edgecumbe and at Sitka High School as well. Her music; her quiet, sincere spirit; and her faithful old van were at the disposal of the church for whatever ministries were needed.

Sybil gave two and a half years of her life to ACTS-TV. She was responsible for laying much of the nitty-gritty groundwork so necessary for a beginning ministry. The behind-the-scenes ministry of this great lady will bear fruit in eternity as ACTS-TV continues across the years. To Sybil and those who supported her financially and with their prayers we are forever indebted.

Another person who deserves much praise and appreciation for the beginning efforts with television production is Larry Hardin.

Larry came to Sheldon Jackson College by an interesting route. In fact, it was because of a call for volunteers made through the facilities of InterCristo in Seattle that he came. Dan Etulain had used this means to advertise for helpers for

Graduation day at Mount Edgecumbe High School with part of Sitka in the background.

ACTS-TV. Since Larry needed support and since the college needed an experienced television person for its educational program, Larry applied for and got the job. But from the beginning his heart was with this ministry which was designed to reach rural Alaska with the Good News.

In the summer of 1982, Larry responded to the promptings of the Holy Spirit to join ACTS-TV full time. This has proved to be a key factor in the ongoing production of programming. You see, Larry is an artist with a television camera and an excellent editor. Without such abilities and skills at our disposal we would be greatly hindered. While his church home is in another denomination his loyalty to the ministry of ACTS-TV is solid and unhindered.

Doubtless one of the most significant developments affecting ACTS-TV is the acquisition of the one commercial television station in Sitka by Dan and Kathie Etulain. This was a giant step of faith for this deeply dedicated couple. It has meant a rearranging of their personal finances so that Dan could spend full time working to develop the station's potential as a commercial Christian family television outlet.

This of course meant that Dan had to terminate his association with Sheldon Jackson College. Kathie's salary at the University of Alaska, Sitka campus, became the support for this young family. This modern-day Priscilla and Aquila are an inspiration to all who know and work with them.

Having the station means more room and equipment available for the production of ACTS-TV. While it is a separate entity, the station contributes to the ministry in significant ways such as bartering for transportation and services with advertisers and offering training to staff members with hands-on experience. Dan envisions the day when KTNL-TV ("Know The Northern Light") will be able to contribute more effectively to the ACTS-TV ministry.

When office space was first needed before the station

was acquired, the Sitka Church of the Nazarene made room in the former garage of the old parsonage.

The door of opportunity for distributing the programming and videotape productions continues to open wider. In 1984 a cable outlet in Anchorage offered time at no cost to ACTS-TV for airing a program a week. This opens up the possibility of reaching the largest concentration of Native Alaskans with the programming.

Serious work is being done on development of Bible study and pastoral training courses which will relate to the Native Alaskan audience. If we are to see the church go beyond its present bases of operation in the larger communities of Alaska we will have to find ways to train Eskimo and Indian leaders in their home villages. Video is one of the most effective and efficient tools for Alaska.

What happens in this far north country could have an impact on other areas in the U.S.A. and Canada where there are concentrated Native North Americans. Could it be in our time to be alive that God is making it possible for us to be a part of a spiritual awakening among a long neglected if not largely forgotten people?

The second verse of a song written by Ruben Hillborn, a Native Alaskan, known as "The Singing Fisherman," aptly sums up the ministry of ACTS-TV. Every year at the Native Musical we recorded the assembled crowd singing their theme:

A NEW LIFE

There is joy within my heart today,
That causes me to sing.
There is peace within my soul today,
That only Christ can bring.
And I'm happy, oh, so happy,
For a new life within,
I'm a child of the King!

Chorus:

A new life, I now know,
And my heart's all aglow.
Trust in Jesus and you'll see
Just how happy life can be.

From the snowy mountaintops
To the deep blue sea,
Across the rolling tundra,
Where the rivers run so free,
I will tell the wondrous story
Of Christ and Calvary.
He means everything to me.

Epilogue

From the City Where They Have No Sun
to
The City Where They Need No Sun

I must open my heart to tell you three more stories from our Alaska experience which illustrate the thoughts I want to leave with you.

In the summer of 1983 while I was working at my desk in the Church Extension Ministries office at the International Headquarters of the Church of the Nazarene in Kansas City, an urgent phone call came.

It was Mary (Oldfriend) Hill—the Eskimo girl who wanted to know if I "do weddings." Mary has kept in touch with us across the years by phone and letter. She said, "Pastor, I thought you would want to know. Liz Cleveland was found shot to death in her home." Mary went on to explain that it looked like a suicide. A thorough investigation was not made. Quinhagak is far from Anchorage, and law enforcement officers do not often get there.

Sometimes I wake up in the night and see the words of her letter before my eyes, "I know you don't want me to give up. I want you, your family, and the Christian people of the Nazarene church to pray for us who are lost in sin, PLEASE!"

I've asked myself a thousand times and more the question, "Did we do all we could do to answer that cry for help?" Sometimes the voice in the night will not be hushed.

In June of 1980 one of my brothers (Donald), his wife (Carol), and their 18-year-old-daughter (Robin) came to Alaska in realization of a long-held dream, to visit us. It was a graduation gift to Robin. The week they were there was historical because there were eight days of sunshine in a row! For a solid week there was not a cloud in the sky! It was an absolutely beautiful time for us all. Cheri and Peter have lived far away from relatives for all their growing-up years. This was the most time they had ever had with a real live cousin.

Peter took them camping, boating, mountain climbing— all the things he dearly loved to do. Cheri and Robin shared things in the way only giggling girls can do.

The evening before they were to leave, we made a home video movie to take back to an anticipated family reunion which would follow the General Assembly.

On a Wednesday evening they caught a delayed Alaska Airlines flight back to Seattle. Upon their arrival there they took off in their own small single-engine plane for a brief flight to Portland, Oreg., and a visit with Carol's family.

Early on Thursday morning of June 12 I received a phone call in the church office that their plane was missing— they had not arrived in Portland as planned. I caught the next flight and traveled a thousand miles south to the area where they were last heard from. Early Friday morning I joined more than 200 search and rescue people in a ground search. The clouds were below the mountain peaks in the beautiful Cascade range about halfway between Mount Rainier and

The Nazarene parsonage in Sitka. Directly behind is the old Russian cemetery.

the recently erupted Mount St. Helens. A thick layer of volcanic dust covered everything, confusing the radio receivers which were homing in on an emergency locater beacon from the missing plane.

Three days after they left Sitka, the wreckage of their plane was sighted by a U.S. Air Force helicopter crew. I was at the radio in the search headquarters when the paramedic who had been lowered to the site reported, "No Survivors."

In my attempts to reconstruct the last moments of that flight, I went to the Seattle-Tacoma Air Traffic Control Center. There I was allowed to listen to the recording of the last five minutes of the radio transmissions between my brother and the traffic controller.

I heard the voice of the pilot reporting that he was encountering low clouds and requesting a change of heading. There was a touch of urgency in his voice that belied his 20 years of flying experience.

The traffic controller responded with the message that

other traffic in the area had priority, and so he said to my pilot-brother, "Stand by." A few minutes later, repeated calls by the traffic controller to the pilot were met by silence.

Five minutes later the flight of Cessna N2335Y was terminated against the side of Mount Griffin.

As I relive that final flight, I am haunted by those words: "STAND BY."

There is no bitterness in my heart about my brother and his family being taken so suddenly. They were all dynamic Christians. Only the Sunday night before their deaths Don had expressed in a testimony from my pulpit in Sitka his feeling from Ps. 16:6: "The lines are fallen unto me in pleasant places; yea, I have a goodly heritage" (KJV). In their quest for a higher altitude they dashed against a stone. God kept His promise and sent angels to bear them up to a much higher altitude.

But the thing that haunts me about the last message that pilot heard is the thought that so many in this my time to be alive are lost in sin's darkness and are calling out in quiet desperation for someone to tell them how to find their way. Too often we answer back that we have other priorities—legitimate and time-consuming.

We too send out the message: "Stand by—we'll get to you later." "Stand by—we're too busy with our own business." "Stand by—we can't help you now." "STAND BY!"

Almost two months to the day after the plane crash, Peter and I stood on top of Mount Edgecumbe. It was the realization of a six-year dream. The first time we laid eyes on that volcanic peak we vowed to climb it. Peter had made one abortive attempt. Bad weather kept the number of successful climbers to a minimum. We wanted to stand on top on a clear day.

So on a Monday noon we made the decision to set out for Kruzof Island, 15 miles across open ocean, in our 13-foot Boston Whaler skiff. From 3 P.M. to 9 P.M. we trudged wearily through soggy muskeg, thick underbrush, up steep slopes and finally, sliding one step back for every two forward, we arrived at the cinder cone top.

It was fabulous! We laid out our sleeping bags under a sky full of stars. Soft moss in hollowed out places in the cinder rock rim of the crater made a perfect mattress.

The next morning the sun coming up over a heavy cloud cover below ended our sleep. While Peter heated water on a backpack stove, I hiked to the edge of the rim to gaze on the fascinating sight of solid clouds separating us from any view of Sitka some 25 miles away. We were alone.

Mount Edgecumbe with the bridge to Japonski Island and Mount Edgecumbe High School in the foreground.

Suddenly our wilderness solitude was interrupted by the cacophony of a helicopter making a sudden appearance over the opposite edge of the crater some mile or so away. We dutifully waved to the tourists who had taken the easy way to the top of the mountain. Only the day before, Cheri had

106

taken a similar flight with a friend in that same helicopter. We felt a little resentment at their intrusion.

As we watched them circle and head toward the opposite edge of the crater for a landing, we were horrified by the sight of pieces of helicopter flying through the air just as they disappeared over the horizon.

In momentary shock we set out at once running toward the site. I grabbed a portable CB radio of questionable power and headed around the crater rim. When I reached a point where I thought there would be no obstructions between me and Sitka I got on the radio and began sending a "Mayday" distress call to anyone who might be listening to whatever channel my CB might have in it. Not having used it for any practical purposes prior to this, I had no idea what frequency I was broadcasting on.

In the meantime, Peter had set a straight course for the crash site which took him down the crater and up the steep bank on the other side. Once again he reached the top before dear old dad.

Much to my great surprise and joy someone answered my call for help. A fisherman in Sitka always kept his radio on and tuned to channel 14—the one I happened to be calling on. He quickly patched me through to the Coast Guard station where a rescue helicopter was warming up on the pad for a routine training flight. So before I reached the top I was talking to the pilot of the rescue chopper who was already headed up through the clouds.

When Peter arrived on the scene, he at first saw no one; he anticipated the worst—that no one had survived. Then as he turned his gaze to the right of the wreckage he saw five people huddled some 200 feet away. Three of them were severely injured, and all were in a state of shock.

To shorten the story, within the hour all five were safely down from the mountain and in the hospital where Mary Jo made their acquaintance and hosted them until they were able to resume their journey. Peter and I remained on the mountain and later in the day made our way back to the cabin at the ocean's edge for the night.

When we told the tourists who we were, while waiting for the Coast Guard to land for the rescue, they requested that we pray for them. There on the mountaintop in the wilderness God gave us a new understanding of Ps. 139:9-10:

> If I take the wings of the dawn,
>> If I dwell in the remotest part of the sea,
> Even there Thy hand will lead me,
>> And Thy right hand will lay hold of me (NASB).

Had the helicopter made its hard landing 10 feet forward or back of where it came down there would have been a thousand-foot tumble from which no one would have survived. Had we not been there at that place and time, it seems certain that shock would have taken its toll, and survival would have been questionable.

When God puts an urge in your heart to climb a mountain, to penetrate a wilderness, to go to a nearby village, He has a reason for your being there.

"God blesses us, that all the ends of the earth may fear Him" (Ps. 67:7, NASB).

Has God blessed you? If so, the only question that remains is, "Which end of the earth, Lord?"